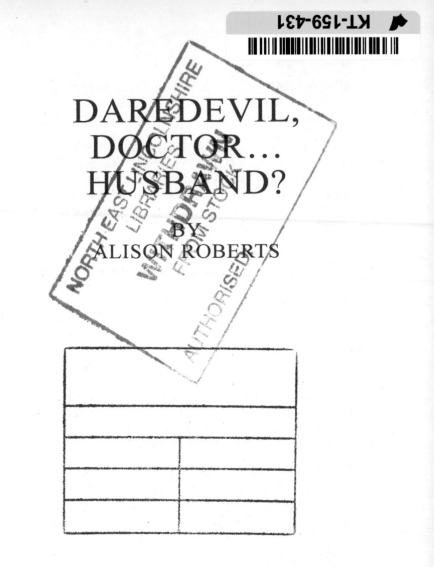

DAREDEVIL, DOCTOR... HUSBAND?

BY
ALISON ROBERTS

MILLS & BOON

First published in Great Britain 2015
By Mills & Boon, an imprint of HarperCollins*Publishers*
1 London Bridge Street, London, SE1 9GF

Large Print edition 2016

ISBN: 978-0-263-26082-3

Our policy is to use papers that are natural, renewable and recyclable products and made from wood grown in sustainable forests. The logging and manufacturing processes conform to the legal environmental regulations of the country of origin.

Printed and bound in Great Britain
by CPI Antony Rowe, Chippenham, Wiltshire

X
3/18

·012   ·A.

'Would you like to come in for a drink or something?'

Summer turned her head as well, and suddenly their faces were too close. She could see the genuine warmth of that invitation in his eyes.

What was the 'something' on offer as well as a drink?

Whatever it was, she wanted it. The attraction was as strong as it was unexpected. She could feel the curl of it deep in her belly. A delicious cramp that eased into tendrils and floated right down to her toes.

She'd been fighting this from the moment she'd first seen the man this morning, hadn't she?

He was—quite simply—gorgeous…

She couldn't look away. Couldn't find anything to say. All she could do was stare at those dark eyes. Feel the puff of his breath on her face. Notice the dark stubble on his jaw and how soft it made his lips look…

Dear Reader,

Sometimes my inspiration for a story comes from something tiny that I see or hear that strikes a chord and keeps resurfacing.

About two years ago I moved from my earthquake-damaged home of the last thirty years in Christchurch to come to New Zealand's biggest city: Auckland. I chose to live on the north side of the harbour bridge and found myself living within walking distance of a beach for the first time in my life. A very beautiful beach—Takapuna.

On a warm night last summer I was on the beach, looking out over a sea as calm as a huge swimming pool, enjoying the silhouette of the volcanic island of Rangitoto, when I saw something that was one of those tiny things: a paddle boarder, quite a long way offshore, who had a big dog along for the ride, lying on the end of his board. It tugged at my heartstrings to recognise the bond they clearly had, and it made me smile every time I remembered.

So that was my starting point. Now come and meet my heroine, Summer, who has a dog called Flint who rides on her board. You'll get to spend some time on Takapuna Beach, too, where my gorgeous hero Zac is lucky enough to live. The sea isn't always calm, of course. And what happens between Zac and Summer isn't either…

Happy reading!

Love

Alison xxx

Alison Roberts lives in Auckland, New Zealand, and has written over sixty Mills & Boon Medical Romance books. As a qualified paramedic she has personal experience of the drama and emotion to be found in the world of medical professionals, and loves to weave stories with this rich background—especially when they can have a happy ending.

When Alison is not writing you'll find her indulging her passion for dancing or spending time with her friends (including Molly the dog) and her daughter Becky, who has grown up to become a brilliant artist. She also loves to travel, hates housework, and considers it a triumph when the flowers outnumber the weeds in her garden.

Books by Alison Roberts

Mills & Boon Medical Romance

Visit the Author Profile page at millsandboon.co.uk for more titles.

CHAPTER ONE

HE WAS NOTHING like what she'd expected.

Well, the fact that he was tall, dark and ridiculously good-looking was no surprise for someone who'd been considered the most eligible doctor at Auckland General Hospital a couple of years ago but Summer Pearson had good reason to believe this man was a total bastard. A monster, even.

And monsters weren't supposed to have warm brown eyes and a smile that could light up an entire room. Maybe she'd made an incorrect assumption when she'd been given the name of her extra crew for the shift.

'Dr Mitchell?'

'That's me.'

'*Zac* Mitchell?'

'Yep. My gran still calls me Isaac, mind you. She doesn't hold with names being messed around with. She's an iceberg lettuce kind of girl, you know? You won't find any of those new-fangled fancy baby mesclun leaves in one of her salads because that's another thing that shouldn't get messed with.'

Good grief...he was telling her about his granny? And there was sheer mischief in those dark eyes. Salad greens and names were clearly only a couple of the many things Zac was more than happy to mess around with. Summer could feel her eyes narrowing as the confirmation of her suspicions became inevitable.

'And you used to work in Auckland? In A&E?'

'Sure did. I've spent the last couple of years in the UK, though. As the permanent doctor on shift for the busiest helicopter rescue service in the country.'

The base manager, Graham, came into the duty room, an orange flight suit draped over his arm.

'Found one in your size, Zac. And here's a tee shirt, too. I see you've met Summer?'

'Ah...we hadn't got as far as a proper introduction.'

Because she'd been grilling him like a prosecution lawyer in a courtroom—making sure of the identity of the accused before firing the real ammunition? Summer felt her cheeks getting pink.

'Sorry,' she muttered. 'I'm Summer Pearson. Intensive Care Paramedic. I've been with the rescue service for nearly three years now.'

'I've heard a lot about you.' An eyebrow lifted and his tone dropped a notch. 'And it was all good.'

No...was he trying to *flirt* with her?

I've heard a lot about you, too. And none of it was good...

Pretending she hadn't heard the compliment, Summer turned to Graham. 'I'll do the usual orientation while we're quiet, shall I?'

A groan came from the doorway as another man entered the room. 'Oh, no...did she just say the Q word?'

'She did.' Graham shook his head. 'What's your guess?'

'Eight minutes.'

'I'll give it six.' Graham grinned at Zac. 'Running bet on how long till a job comes in after someone says the Q word. Worst performer of the week restocks the beer fridge. Meet Monty, Zac—one of our pilots.'

The men shook hands. Then they all looked at Summer and she tried to erase the expression that felt remarkably like a scowl from her face.

'Three minutes,' she offered reluctantly. Wishful thinking, maybe, but how good would it be if what was likely to be a complicated winch job came in and an untrained doctor had to be left on base in favour of experienced crewmen? 'So I guess we'd better get started on the orientation.'

'Just show him where everything is,' Graham said. 'Zac, here, is the most highly trained doctor we've ever had joining us. Fully winch trained. He's done HUET and he's even part way through his pilot's training.'

Summer could feel the scowl creeping back. She refused to be impressed but it was difficult. Helicopter Underwater Escape Training was not something for the faint-hearted.

Zac was shrugging off the praise. 'I'm passionate about emergency medicine, that's all. And the challenge of being on the front line is a lot more exciting than working inside a controlled environment like an emergency department. Maybe I haven't really grown up yet, and that keeps me chasing adventures.'

Immaturity was no excuse for anything. It certainly didn't mitigate ruining someone's life and then walking away. Summer tried to catch Graham's eye. Could she tell him she really wasn't comfortable working with this new team member?

She didn't get the chance. The strident signal from the on-base communication system told them a job had come in.

Monty checked his watch. 'Two minutes, ten seconds. You win, Summer.'

She picked up her helmet and jammed it on her head. She didn't feel as if she'd won anything at all.

She was nothing like what he'd expected.

Well, she *was* small. No more than about five

foot four at a guess. Her head barely reached his shoulder and that was including the spikes of her short blonde hair. *Pocket rocket,* his ED colleagues had told him. *But don't be fooled. She's as tough as. And one of the best paramedics in the business.*

But they'd also told him she was Summer by name and sunny by nature. And that she was great fun to work with. *You're a lucky man,* they'd said.

He'd been expecting summer and he'd got winter instead. Funny, but he didn't feel that lucky.

Or maybe he did. Here he was in a chopper again and he hadn't realised how much he was missing the excitement of being airborne and heading for the unknown. Not only that, he was doing it over the sparkling blue waters of his home town instead of the grey British skies he'd become so familiar with. And they were heading for even more spectacular scenery on the far side of the Coromandel Peninsula—one of his most favourite places on earth.

'Car's over a bank,' he heard through the speakers built into his helmet. 'On the 309, between the Kauri grove and Waiau Falls. Ambulance and fire service are on scene.'

'The 309's still a gravel road, I presume?'

'You know it?' Monty sounded surprised.

'Spent most of my childhood holidays on the Coromandel. I'm into water sports.'

'Talk to Summer.' Monty chuckled. 'Queen of the paddleboard, she is.'

Zac would have been happy to do exactly that but it only took a glance to see that she had no desire to chat. Her face was turned away and she gave the impression of finding the view too fascinating to resist.

She still looked small, with the wide straps of her harness across her chest. The helmet looked too big for her head and while someone might be excused for getting the impression of a child playing dress-up, they'd only need to see her profile to sense a very adult level of focus and…what was it…judgement?

Yeah… He felt as if he'd been tried and judged and the verdict had not been favourable.

But he'd never even met the woman before today so what was he being judged on?

Was she some kind of control freak, perhaps, who didn't appreciate having someone on board who had a medical authority higher than hers? Or did she require confirmation that a newcomer's ability was what it appeared to be on paper?

Fair enough.

What wasn't acceptable was making said newcomer feel less than welcome. Undesirable, even.

As if she felt the force of his frown, Summer turned her head. Her gaze met his and held longer than could be considered polite.

Yeah...she was fierce, all right. Unafraid.

Who was going to look away first? Defusing tension was a skill that came automatically for Zac. He might have had to learn it for all the wrong reasons when he was too young to understand but shades of that ability still came in handy at times. All it usually took was turning on the charm. He summoned his best smile and, for a split second, he thought it was going to work because she almost smiled back. But then she jerked her head, breaking the eye contact.

A deliberate snub? Zac tamped down a response that could have been disappointment. Or possibly annoyance. Neither would be helpful in establishing a good working relationship with this unexpectedly prickly young woman.

'You should get a good view of the Pinnacles on your side in a few minutes,' Summer said.

'Might get a bit bumpy going over the mountains,' Monty added. 'I'll get an update on scene info as soon as we get over the top.'

When he'd first started this kind of work, Zac would be using this time to go over all the possible medical scenarios in his head and the procedures that might be needed to deal with them. A chest decompression for a pneumothorax, perhaps. Management of a spinal, crush or severe head injury. Partial or complete amputations. Uncontrollable haemorrhage. But the list was long and he'd learned that there was no point expending mental energy on imaginary scenarios.

He'd also learned that it was better to start a

job without assumptions that could distract him from the unexpected. And that he could deal with whatever he found. This time was better used to relax and centre himself. The view of the spectacular bush-covered peaks below them was ideal—and definitely better than trying to make conversation with someone who clearly had no intention of making his life any more pleasant.

'ETA two minutes.'

'Roger.' Summer leaned forward in her seat to get a better view of the ground below. 'Vehicles at eleven o'clock. I can see a fire truck and ambulance.'

'Copy that,' Monty said. 'Comms? Rescue One. On location, on location.'

The chopper tilted as they turned. Monty was using the crew frequency now. 'Turning windward,' he advised. 'I think the road's going to be the only landing place.'

'Got a bit of a tilt to it. No wires, though.'

'No worries,' Monty said. 'Be a bit dusty, folks. Okay…right skid's going to touch first.'

They had the doors open before the dust cloud had cleared. Zac released the catch of his safety harness first and hoisted one of the backpacks onto his shoulder as they climbed out.

Summer picked up the other pack and a portable oxygen cylinder and followed. Weirdly, it felt like she was used to working with this guy already. Maybe that was because he seemed to know exactly what he was doing and he wasn't waiting to follow her lead. At least he stood back when they reached the knot of people standing by the side of the road near the fire truck so it was Summer that the fireman in charge of the scene spoke to first.

'We've got the vehicle secured but haven't got the driver out. It's a bit of a steep climb.'

'Single occupant?'

'Yes. An eighty-three-year-old woman. Frances.'

'Status?'

'I'd say two.' An ambulance officer joined them. 'GCS was lowered on arrival. She's confused and distressed. Airway seems to be clear but we haven't got close enough to assess her properly yet and, given the MOI and her age, there's every probability she has serious injuries.'

'Access?'

'Ladder. It's a few metres short of the target, though. You'll have to be careful but there's plenty of trees to hang on to.'

'Cool. We'll go down and see what's what.' Summer glanced at Zac. Tall and broad-shouldered, his size and weight would make the climb and access to the vehicle much harder than it was for her. It would probably be sensible for him to suggest waiting up here on the road while she did an initial assessment and made their patient stable enough to be extricated by the fire crew.

'Want me to go first?' he asked. 'And test the ladder?'

'If you like.' Summer passed her backpack to a fireman who was ready to secure it to a rope and lower it down. Not that it was needed, but she had to give him points for thinking about her safety.

Looking at the narrow ladder lying on the crushed and probably slippery ferns of the bush undergrowth on an almost vertical cliff face, she had to acknowledge those points.

'Yeah…you going first is a good idea, Zac. There'll be less damage done if I land on you rather than the other way round.'

'Impersonating a cushion is one of my splinter skills.' Zac handed his pack to the fireman and then turned without hesitation to climb onto the ladder. A rope attached to the top and anchored to the back of the fire truck was preventing it sliding downwards but it couldn't control any sideways movement. Another rope was attached to the back of the small car that could be seen protruding from the mangled scrub and ferns a good fifteen metres down the bank.

'She was lucky the scrub cushioned the impact,' the fireman said. 'Probably why she's still alive.'

Zac was halfway down the ladder now and climbing carefully enough not to make it swing. Summer caught the top rung and turned her body to find a foothold. She loved the kind of challenge this sort of job presented. The ladder was easy.

Getting down the last stretch when you had to slide between trees was harder. There were fire crew down here but it was Zac who was moving just ahead of her and every time he caught himself, he was looking back to make sure she'd reached her last handhold safely.

It was Summer who needed to take the lead as they got close enough to touch the car. A small hatchback well buried in undergrowth left virtually no room for a large man to see much. The front passenger window had been smashed. Summer put her head in the gap.

'Hi there...Frances, is it?'

The elderly woman groaned. Her voice was high and quavery. 'Get me out. *Please*...'

'That's what we're here for. My name's Summer and I've got Zac with me. Are you having any trouble breathing, Frances?'

'I...I don't think so.'

'Does anything hurt?'

'I...I don't know...I'm *scared*...'

Summer was trying to assess their patient visually. Pale skin and a bump on the head that was bleeding. She could see the woman's chest rising and falling rapidly. The more distressed she was, the harder it would be to assess and try to move her.

The window on the driver's side was broken too and suddenly there was movement as the prickly branches of scrub got pushed aside. The face that appeared was wearing a helmet. How on earth had Zac managed to get down that side of the vehicle?

Not only that, he was reaching in to touch the woman. To put a calming hand on her forehead, probably to stop her turning her head to look at him in case she had injured her neck.

'It's okay, sweetheart,' he said. 'We're going to take good care of you.'

Sweetheart? Was that an appropriate way to address an eighty-three-year-old woman?

'Oh…' Frances didn't seem offended. 'Oh… Who are you?'

'I'm Zac. I'm a doctor.'

'Do I know you?'

'You do now.' He leaned in further, a lopsided

smile appearing as he make a clicking sound like someone encouraging a pony to move. The sound was accompanied by a wink.

'Oh...' The outward breath sounded like a sigh of relief. There was even a shaky smile in response. 'Thank you, dear. I've been *so* scared...'

'I know.' His voice was understanding. Reassuring. Was he holding a hand or taking a pulse in there? 'Summer—are you able to open the door on your side? It's jammed over here.'

With the assistance of a fireman and a crowbar, the answer was affirmative.

With the new space, Summer was able to ease herself cautiously into the car. The creaking and slight forward movement of the vehicle made her catch her breath but it terrified Frances.

'*No...help...*'

This time it was Summer as well as their patient who took comfort from Zac's confident tone. 'The ropes just needed to take up the extra weight. You're safe. There's a great big fire engine up on the road that's not going anywhere and the car is very firmly attached to it. Relax, sweetheart...'

There it was again. That cheeky endearment. Summer wouldn't want to admit that skip of her heart when it seemed like the car was beginning to roll further down the cliff. She most definitely wouldn't want to admit that warm feeling the use of the endearment created. How powerful could a single word be? It could make you think that someone genuinely cared about you.

That you were, indeed, safe.

Suddenly, it was easy to focus completely on the job she needed to do. Summer unhooked the stethoscope from around her neck and fitted it into her ears.

'Take a deep breath for me, Frances.'

There was equal air entry in both lungs and a pulse that was a little too fast and uneven enough to suggest an underlying cardiac condition, although Frances denied having any. The worst bleeding from lacerations in papery skin needed pressure dressings for control because blood pressure was already low and Summer eased a cervical collar in place as Zac held the head steady.

'Sorry, Frances. I know this is uncomfortable but it's to protect your neck while we get you out. We can't examine you properly until we get you up to the ambulance.'

'That's all right, dear.' But it was Zac that Frances was looking at for reassurance. His hand she was holding through the window as Summer worked quickly beside her in the car.

'Are you sure nothing's hurting, Frances?'

'My chest is a bit sore. And my arm...'

'We can give you something for the pain.'

But Frances shook her head. 'I can bear it, dear. It's not that bad...'

Summer glanced up at Zac, who was still supporting the elderly woman's head and neck. 'We can reassess after we move her but I think we can probably wait till we get up to the top before worrying about IV access.'

'Absolutely.' Zac nodded. 'The tubing and trying to carry a bag of fluids will only create a complication we don't need. Bit of oxygen might be a good idea, though, do you think?'

'Sure.'

They explained how they were going to get her out of the car, using a backboard to slide her towards the passenger side and then turning her to lie flat as they lifted her out onto a stretcher.

'You'll be quite safe,' Summer said. 'We've got lots of strong young firemen to carry you up the hill.'

'Oh…I've caused everybody so much trouble, haven't I?'

'It's what we do,' Zac told her. 'If people didn't have accidents or get sick, we'd be out of a job.' He was smiling again. 'And we *love* our job, don't we, Summer?'

This time, she really couldn't help smiling back so she tilted her head towards her patient. 'Indeed we do. Okay, Frances. You ready to get out of here?'

Getting her out of the car had to be done as gently as possible because there could be fractured bones or internal injuries that hadn't been recognised due to position and limited access but if there had been any increase in pain during the procedure, Frances wasn't complaining. Cocooned in a blanket and strapped securely into the Stokes basket stretcher, she looked almost relaxed as the rescue team began the slow process of inching the stretcher up to the road.

In the relative safety of the ambulance, it was Zac who led a more complete examination while an ambulance officer filled in some paperwork.

'Next of kin?'

'I haven't got any. Not now.'

'Is there anyone you'd like us to call?'

'Maybe my neighbour. She'll take care of the cats if I don't get home tonight. Oh...that's why I was driving today. There's a special on in the supermarket at Whitianga. For cat food.'

Zac got an IV line through fragile skin with a skill that was unlikely to leave so much as a bruise and Summer hooked up the IV fluids, aware of how meticulous and gentle the rest of his survey was, despite being rapid enough to get them on their way as soon as possible. ECG electrodes, blood pressure and oxygen saturation monitors were in place and Zac was keeping an eye on all the readings. A raised eyebrow at Summer had her nodding. The heart rhythm wasn't dangerous but was definitely abnormal and would need treatment.

'You don't get dizzy spells, do you, Frances?' Zac asked. 'You weren't feeling sick before the accident?'

'I don't think so. I really can't remember...'

'What medications are you on?'

'I don't take anything, dear. Apart from my calcium tablets. I'm as healthy as a horse. Haven't needed to see a doctor for years.'

'Might be a good thing that you're going to get a proper check-up in hospital then. Bit of a warrant of fitness.'

'I don't like bothering a doctor when I don't need to.'

'I know. My gran Ivy is exactly the same.'

'How old is *she*?'

'Ninety-two.'

Summer found herself sliding a quizzical

glance in his direction as she gathered dressings and bandages to dress some of the superficial wounds more thoroughly. It wouldn't occur to her to think about, let alone tell others, anything about her own family. What was it with him and his grandmother? Nobody could miss the pride in his voice and it just didn't fit with the whole cheeky, bad boy vibe. And it certainly didn't fit with his reputation.

'She still swims every day,' Zac added. 'Has done her whole life. Reckons she's half-mermaid. Does it hurt if I press here?'

'Ooh...yes...'

'Can you wiggle your fingers?'

'That hurts, too... Have I broken something?'

'It's possible. We'll put a splint on it and keep it nice and still till you get an X-ray. We might give you something for the pain, too. You don't have to be brave and put up with it, you know. Sometimes, it's nice to just let someone else take care of you.'

Frances got a bit weepy at that point but the

transfer to the helicopter and their take-off a short time later was enough of a distraction.

It didn't quite distract Summer. Was Frances stoic and uncomplaining because there was no point in being anything else? Was there really nobody who needed to know she'd had a bad accident other than her neighbour?

The thought was sad.

Maybe more so because it resonated. As the chopper lifted and swung inland to head back to Auckland, Summer watched the people on the ground get smaller and a cluster of houses in the small township of Coromandel where Frances lived become visible. They vanished just as quickly and Summer turned, wondering if the elderly woman was aware and distressed by how far from her home they were taking her.

'Morphine's doing its job.' Zac's voice sounded loud in her helmet. 'She's having a wee nap.' His eyes were on the cardiac monitor. 'She's stable. Enjoy the view.'

But Summer still felt oddly flat. What if she'd been the one to have an accident in such an isolated location? Who would she call if she was about to be flown to an emergency department a long way from her home?

It was moments like this that she noticed the absence of a partner in her life with a sharpness that felt increasingly like failure since she'd entered her thirties and everyone her age seemed to be getting married and starting families. There was nobody to call her 'sweetheart' and really mean it. No one to make her feel cherished and safe. It wasn't that she hadn't tried to find someone—relationships just never seemed to work out.

If she was really honest, though, she hadn't tried that hard. She'd told herself that there was plenty of time and her career had to take priority but it went deeper than that, didn't it? Moments like this always made the loss of her mother seem like yesterday instead of more than fifteen years ago and what she'd been taught about not trusting men was as much a part of those memories as anything else.

Would she put her father down as next of kin?

Not likely. She hadn't seen him since her mother's funeral and there was still anger there that he'd had the nerve to turn up for it.

She'd probably do what Frances had done and opt to put a call in to a neighbour to make sure her pet was cared for.

No. Her life wasn't that sad. She had a lot of good friends. The guys she worked with, for starters. And her oldest friend, Kate, would do anything to help. It was just a shame she lived in Hamilton—a good hour's drive away. Not that that was any excuse for the fact they hadn't seen each other for so long. Or even talked, come to that.

And, boy…they had something to talk about now, didn't they?

With Zac monitoring Frances during the flight and clearly happy that the condition of their patient was still stable, there was no reason why Summer shouldn't get her mobile phone from her pocket and flick off a text message.

Hey, Kate. How's things? U home tonite?

The response came back swiftly.

Late finish but home by 10. Call me. Be good 2 talk.

It would. Her friend might need some prior warning, though.

You'll never guess who's back in town!

CHAPTER TWO

'ZAC…WHEN DID you get back into town?' The nurse wheeling an IV trolley through the emergency department was overdoing the delighted astonishment just a tad when she caught sight of the helicopter crew coming out of Resus.

'Only last week. Didn't see you around, Mandy.'

'I was on holiday. Giving my new bikini a test run on a beach in Rarotonga.'

'Nice.'

'It was. Is. Pink—with little purple flowers. Might have to give it another outing at Takapuna on my next day off.'

It was no surprise that Mandy chose to assume he was referring to the bikini rather than the Pacific island. Confident and popular, she had flirting down to a fine art. There were rumours that it went further than flirting but Summer preferred to trust her own instincts and Mandy had always been willing to help when their paths crossed at work and good company at social events. The smile was as friendly as ever right now, but somehow it struck a discordant note. Maybe it had been the tone in Zac's voice. Or the warm glance that had flashed between them.

No surprise there, so why was it so annoying?

Because her instincts had been trying to convince her that Zac wasn't the monster she'd heard about? That someone who could treat a frightened elderly patient as if she was his own beloved granny couldn't possibly be that bad? They'd just finished handing Frances over to the team in Resus and Zac had promised to come and visit to see how she was as soon as he was back in the department again. There had been tears on her wrinkled cheeks as she'd told Rob, the ED consultant taking over, that this 'dear boy' had saved her life.

'That's our Zac.' Rob had grinned. 'We're lucky to have him back but we're letting him out to play on the helicopters every so often.'

It was a reminder that she was on Zac's turf now because his primary job was as another one of the department's consultants. After three years of working in Auckland, both on the road and in the rescue service, Summer felt as much at home in this environment as she did on station or at the base but something subtle had just shifted in unspoken ratings. Zac was the person Frances considered to be her lifesaver. He was also a doctor and clearly not only respected for his skills but well liked. Probably more popular than Mandy, even?

Did none of them know what she knew about him?

She'd been close to doubting the truth herself but seeing the way he and Mandy had looked at each other was a wake-up call. She'd been in danger of being sucked in by that charm. Like countless other women, including Mandy. And Kate's sister, Shelley. Had she really been prepared to dismiss how Shelley's life had been wrecked?

'Hey, Summer.' Mandy was still smiling. 'Have you guys stolen Zac away from us?'

'Wouldn't dream of it.' She kept her tone light enough for her words to pass as a joke. 'I'm sure he'll get sick of us soon enough and he'll be all yours again.'

Mandy's sigh was theatrical. 'Dreams are free,' she murmured.

A curtain twitched open nearby. 'We need that trolley, Mandy. When you're ready?'

'Oops.' Mandy rolled her eyes, blew a kiss in Zac's direction and disappeared with her trolley.

It was only then that Summer felt the stare she was receiving. A level stare. Cool enough to be a completely different season from a few seconds ago when Mandy had been present.

Had he guessed that she hadn't been joking? That she'd been wishful thinking out loud? Did she care?

No.

Then why was she suddenly feeling like a complete bitch? Helicopter crews were notoriously tight teams. They had to be. This was Zac's first day on the job and, under any other circumstances, he would be a welcome addition to the team. Perfect, in fact. She'd never gone out of her way to make a newcomer feel unwelcome. Ever.

She got a glimpse of how she must be coming across to Zac and she didn't like what she saw.

And that was even more annoying than feeling as if she had a running battle between her head and heart about what sort of person he really was. Or watching him confirm his 'bad boy' reputation by encouraging Mandy.

Summer was being someone she didn't even recognise.

'We'd better take this stretcher back upstairs. Monty'll be wondering where we've got to.' She couldn't meet his gaze any longer. Was this unfamiliar, unpleasant sensation what it felt like to be ashamed of yourself? She needed to find some way to rectify the situation. But how?

She manoeuvred the stretcher into the lift. They would be airborne again within minutes, either on their way back to base or onto another job. They had to work together so, at the very least, she had to be professional and to stop letting anything personal get in the way of that.

She broke the awkward silence in the lift just before the doors opened at roof level. 'Great job, by the way...with Frances.'

Talk about being damned by faint praise.

And she'd all but announced to Mandy that she'd be delighted if he decided he'd rather stay within the four walls of the hospital's emergency department from now on. How long would it take for that message to get dispersed amongst his colleagues?

He'd been looking forward to this. Coming into the department as a uniformed HEMS member to hand over his first patient. Showing everybody that this was where his passion lay and that he was good at it. This was supposed to be the start of the life he'd dreamed of. A job that used every ounce of skill he possessed and challenged him to keep learning more. A balance of the controlled safety of a state-of-the-art emergency department with the adrenaline rush of coping with the un-expected in sometimes impossible environments. The chance to do exactly the job he wanted in the place he'd always wanted to do it in—close to the only family he had, in a city big enough to offer everything, a great climate and, best of all, the sea within easy reach. Beaches and boats. The perfect playground to unwind in after giving your all at work.

But the blue sky of that promise of fulfilment had a big cloud in it. A dark cloud that threatened rain. Possibly even hail and thunder.

How ironic was it that her name was Summer?

'Yes?'

Oh, Lord…had he said something out loud? The microphone on his helmet was so close to his mouth, it could easily pick something up, even with the increasing roar of the rotors picking up speed to take off. Like the ironic tone of her name. He had to think fast.

'Cute name,' he offered. 'Can't say I've ever met a Summer before.'

'My parents were hippies. Apparently I got conceived on a beach. After a surfing competition.'

Monty's laugh reminded him that this conversation wasn't private. 'I never knew that. No wonder you've got sea water in your veins.'

It was the first piece of personal information Summer had offered. Monty's amusement added to a lighter atmosphere and Zac wanted more.

'A summer memory to keep, then?'

'Yeah...'

'Not many people know where they were conceived. I wouldn't have a clue.'

'Maybe you should ask your mother.'

'My mother died in a car accident when I was seven and I never knew my dad. I got brought up by my gran.'

'Oh...' She caught his gaze for a moment, horrified that she'd been so insensitive. 'Sorry...'

'No worries. It's ancient history.' Zac was happy to keep the conversation going. 'You got any siblings? Spring, maybe? Or Autumn?'

'Nope.'

The word was a snap. She could offer personal information but he wasn't welcome to ask for it.

Zac suppressed a sigh. Maybe he should have

a word to the base manager about being assigned to a different shift on the rescue service.

The call coming in meant that wasn't going to happen any time soon.

'Missing child,' Comms relayed. 'Six-year-old boy. Red tee shirt, blue shorts, bare feet. They think he's been swept off rocks at St Leonard's beach. Coastguard's sending a boat and the police chopper's on its way but you're closest.'

A six-year-old boy.

How long would he last in the water? How frightened would he be?

He was close to the same age Zac had been when he'd lost his mother. Summer could only imagine how frightened *he* would have been. He would have had the same soft dark curls by then. And big brown eyes.

Heart-wrenching.

She didn't want to feel sorry for Zac, any more than she wanted his charm to get under her skin.

Maybe this kid could swim. She'd been able to at least keep herself afloat by the time she was four but Monty was right—she had sea water in her veins and life had been all about the sun and sand and surf back then. Happy days.

They were circling above the cliffs and rocks surrounding one of the many bays on Auckland's north shore now and she could see the knot of people anxiously staring at the sea. Others were climbing the rocks, staring down into the pools where a small body could wash up with the incoming tide. In the distance, as they circled again, she could see a coastguard boat leaving a foamy wake behind it as it sped out from the inner harbour.

Her heart was sinking. It was too hard to keep feeling optimistic that this search would have a happy ending.

And one glance at how pale Zac was looking, with that fierce frown of deep concern on his face, and it was too hard to keep believing that he was some kind of monster.

Round and round they went. Monty focused on keeping them low and moving slowly over a small area, his crew peering down, trying to spot the smallest sign of anything in the soft blue swells of water or the whiteness as they broke over rocks.

Emergency vehicles were gathering at a nearby park above the beach. A police car and then a fire engine. An ambulance...

'What was that?'

'Where?'

'I think I caught a flash of something red.'

'*Where?*' Summer narrowed her eyes, willing something to show up on the water below. The coastguard boat was there now. And a civilian dinghy. Even someone on a paddleboard.

'Not in the water. Up the cliff. Take us round again, Monty.'

Another slow circuit but Summer couldn't see anything.

'I swear I saw it. About halfway up, where that pohutukawa tree is coming out sideways.'

Monty stopped their circling and hovered. Took them in a bit closer. A bit lower.

'*There*...' Excitement made Zac's voice reverberate in her helmet. 'Two o'clock. There's a bit of an overhang behind the trunk. There's something there. Something *red...*'

They hovered where they were as the information was relayed to emergency crews on the ground. A fire truck got shifted and parked at the top of the cliff, facing backwards. Abseiling gear and a rope appeared and then someone was on their way down to check out the possible sighting. For an agonisingly long moment, the fire officer disappeared after climbing over the trunk and crawling beneath the overhang.

Summer held her breath.

He reappeared, backing out slowly so it took another couple of seconds to see that he held something in his arms. A small child, wearing a red T-shirt and shorts. And then he held up his hand and, despite the heavy gloves he was wearing, it was clear that he was giving a 'thumbs-up' signal that all was well.

The boy was not injured.

The relief was surprisingly overwhelming. It was instinctive to share that relief with someone, as if sharing would somehow confirm that what she was seeing was real. Maybe Zac felt the same way because their eyes met at precisely the same instant.

And, yes…her own relief was reflected there. Zac had probably dealt with the same kind of heart-breaking jobs she had in the past, where a child's life had been lost. The kind of jobs you would choose never to repeat if it was within your power—something they both knew was too much to hope for. But this time they'd won. The boy's family had won. Tragedy had been averted and it felt like a major triumph.

The momentary connection was impossible to dismiss. She and Zac felt exactly the same way and the depth of a bond that came from the kind of trauma that was part of what they did was not something everybody could share. Even amongst colleagues, the ability to distance yourself from feeling so strongly was very different. Summer still couldn't breathe past the huge lump in her throat and she suspected that Zac was just the same.

But he wasn't supposed to have an emotional

connection to others like this, given what Summer knew about him. It was confusing. Not to be trusted.

The radio message telling the rescue crew to stand down broke the atmosphere. Monty's delighted whoop as he turned away and swept them back towards base added a third person to the mix and suddenly it became purely professional again and not at all confusing.

'How lucky was that?' They could hear the grin in Monty's voice. 'The kid decided to go climbing instead of getting washed out to sea.'

'Small boys can climb like spiders.'

'Only going up, though. It's when it's time to go down that they realise they're stuck.'

'He must have been scared stiff,' Summer put in. 'Good thing there was the overhang to climb under.'

'He probably knew he'd be in trouble. No wonder he decided it was safer to hide for a while.'

'He won't be in trouble.' Zac's voice was quiet. 'Or not for long, anyway. I'd love to have seen his mum's face when she gets to give him a hug.'

This time, Summer deliberately didn't look at Zac but kept her gaze on the forest of masts in the yacht marina below. She didn't want to see the recognition of what it was like to know you'd lost someone precious and what a miracle it would be to have them returned to you. Zac must have dreamed of such a miracle when he was the same age as that little boy in the red tee shirt. How long had it taken to understand that it was never going to happen?

She'd known instantly. Did that make it easier?

If she'd met his gaze, it might be a question that was impossible not to ask silently and maybe she didn't want to know the answer because that might extend that connection she'd felt.

A connection that felt wrong.

Almost like a betrayal of some kind?

Life didn't get much better than this.

A quiet, late summer evening on Takapuna beach, with a sun-kissed Rangitoto island as a backdrop to a calm blue sea. The long swim had been invigorating and it was still warm enough to sit and be amongst so many people enjoying themselves. There weren't many people swimming now but there were lots of small boats coming in to the ramp at the end of the beach, paddleboarders beyond where the gentle waves were breaking and people walking their dogs. A group of young men were having a game of football and family groups were picnicking on the nearby grassed area.

It was the kind of scene that was so much a part of home for Zac he'd missed it with an ache during his years in London. This beach had been his playground for as long as he could remember. He loved it in all its moods—as calm as an oversized swimming pool some days, wild and stormy and leaving a mountain of seaweed on the beach at other times. Little room to walk at high tide but endless sand and rocks to clamber over at low tide. Kite surfers loved it on the windy days and paddleboards reigned on days like this.

Funny that he'd never tried that particular water sport. Maybe because it looked a bit tame. For heaven's sake—it was so tame, there was somebody out there with a dog sitting behind the person who was standing, paddling the board.

A big dog. A small person. They were attracting attention from some of the walkers and Zac could see the pleasure they were getting from the sight by the way they were pointing and smiling. More than one person was capturing the image with a camera. He took another look himself. The dog was shaggy and black. The paddler was a girl in a bikini and even from this distance she was clearly attractively curvy.

He'd finished rubbing himself down with his towel so there was no reason not to head back to the house for a hot shower but there was still enough warmth in the setting sun to make it pleasant to stand here and that pleasure certainly wasn't dimmed by watching the girl on the paddleboard for a few more moments as she headed in to shore. How would the dog cope with the challenge of staying on board as they negotiated even small waves?

It didn't. As soon as the board began to ride the swell, it jumped clear and swam beside its owner, who stayed upright and rode in until the board beached itself on the sand. It was only then that Zac realised who he'd been watching.

What had Monty called her?

Oh, yeah...the queen of the paddleboard.

Who knew that that flight suit had been covering curves that were all the sweeter when there wasn't an ounce of extra flesh anywhere else on her body? The muscles in her arms and legs had the kind of definition that only peak fitness could maintain and she had a six-pack that put his to shame.

Zac found himself sucking in his stomach just a little as he moved towards where she was dragging the huge board out of the final wash of the waves. He couldn't pretend he hadn't seen her and maybe this was a great opportunity to get past that weird hostility he'd been so aware of today. There'd been a moment when he'd thought it was behind them—when they'd shared that moment of triumph that they no longer needed to try and spot a small body floating in the sea—but it hadn't lasted. Summer had been immersed in paperwork when he'd signed off for his first shift and she'd barely acknowledged his departure.

He summoned a friendly smile. 'Need a hand?'

'*Zac...*'

He was possibly the last person Summer might have expected to meet here on the beach. The last person she would have *wanted* to meet? She was having to share yet another patch of her turf. First the base where she worked. Then the emergency department that was also part of her working life. Now this—not exactly her home but a huge part of when she spent her downtime and a place that was very special to her. And he was... he was almost *naked*.

Oh...my... The board shorts were perfectly respectable attire for the beach but the last time she'd seen him as he left the base that afternoon he'd been wearing real clothes. Clothes that covered up that rather overwhelming expanse of well tanned, smooth, astonishingly *male* skin. He'd obviously towelled himself off recently but droplets of water were still clinging in places. Caught in the sparse hair, for example, between the dark copper discs of his nipples.

'I've been swimming.'

Oh, help... He'd noticed her looking, hadn't he? Hastily, Summer dragged her gaze upwards again. His hair was wet and spiky and his expression suggested that he was as disconcerted as she was by their lack of clothing. Suddenly, it struck her as funny and she had to smile.

'No...really?'

'I'd offer you my towel but it's a bit damp.'

'I've been standing up. I'm not actually that wet.'

Just as she spoke, her dog emerged from his frolic in the waves, bounded towards them, stopped and then shook himself vigorously. It was like a short, sharp and rather cold shower.

'*Flint...* Oh, sorry about that. My bag's just over here. I've got a dry towel in there.'

'No worries.' Zac was laughing. He reached out his hand. 'Hey, Flint...'

The big dog sniffed the hand cautiously, wagged a shaggy tail politely and then sat on the sand, close enough to lean on Summer's leg. He looked up and the question might as well have been a bubble in the air over his head.

Friend of yours? Acceptable company?

Summer touched the dog's head.

Yes. He's okay. I'm safe.

Maybe it was the genuine laughter that had made a joke of something many people would have found annoying. Or the way he'd reached out to make friends with Flint. She might not let people *too* close but she'd always trusted her instincts about their character and there was nothing here to be ringing alarm bells. Quite the opposite, in fact.

'So, do you need a hand dragging this thing somewhere? It looks heavy.'

'No. Jay'll come and get it soon. He's busy giving someone a lesson at the moment.' Turning the board sideways on the soft sand close to her brightly coloured beach bag, she sat down on one end. 'I'll just look after the board until he's done.'

'Jay?'

'He runs a paddleboard business. I hired one

the first time I came to this beach and fell in love with it. I've been coming back ever since.'

'And Flint? He fell in love with it too?' Zac sat down, uninvited, on the other end of the board but somehow it felt perfectly natural. Welcome, even.

'He was in love with me.' The memory made Summer smile. 'Jay was going to look after him while I went for a ride, the first time I brought him here as a pup, but Flint wasn't having any of it. He just came after me. Luckily, Jay shouted loud enough for me to hear so I could fish him out of the water before he got so exhausted he sank. He fell asleep on the board coming back in and that's been his spot ever since.' She laughed. 'You're sitting on it right now. That's why he's standing there glaring at you.'

'Oh...my apologies.' Zac shuffled closer to Summer and Flint stepped onto the end of the board, turned around and then lay down in a neat ball with his nose on his paws.

Zac was so close to Summer now that she could feel the warmth of his skin. His *bare* skin. His legs were bent and she could see sand caught in the dusting of dark hair. The legs of his board shorts were loose enough to be exposing skin on his inner thigh that looked paler than the rest of him. Soft…

She cleared her throat as she looked away. Maybe that would clear inappropriate thoughts as well. 'So why Takapuna? Auckland's got a lot of beaches to choose from when you need an after-work dip.'

'It's been my backyard for ever. That's my gran's house up there.' He was pointing to the prestigious row of houses that had gardens blending into the edge of the beach. Multi-million-dollar houses. 'The old one, with the boat shed and the anchor set in the gate.'

It was impossible not to be seriously impressed. 'You *live* there?'

'I know…' Zac pushed his wet hair off his face. 'It's a bit weird. I'm thirty-six years old and I'm still living with my gran. But the house is on two levels. Gran's upstairs and I rent the bottom half and it's always just worked for both of us. She'd deny it but I think she's relieved to have me back. I'm relieved too, I have to admit. I worried about her while I was away. She's a bit old to be living entirely on her own.'

'A *bit* old? Didn't you say she was in her nineties?'

'Ninety-two. You wouldn't think so, though, if you met her. She reckons ninety is the new seventy.' Zac turned his head. 'She'd love to meet you. Would you like to come in for a drink or something?'

Summer turned her head as well and suddenly their faces were too close. She could see the genuine warmth of that invitation in his eyes. What was the 'something' on offer as well as a drink?

Whatever it was, she wanted it. The attraction was as strong as it was unexpected. She could feel the curl of it deep in her belly. A delicious cramp that eased into tendrils that floated right down to her toes.

She'd been fighting this from the moment she'd first seen this man this morning, hadn't she?

He was—quite simply—gorgeous...

It wasn't just his looks. It was his enthusiasm for his work. His charm. That smile. The way he loved his grandmother.

She couldn't look away. Couldn't find anything to say. All she could do was stare at those dark eyes. Feel the puff of his breath on her face. Notice the dark stubble on his jaw and how soft it made his lips look…

The board beneath her rocked a little as Flint jumped off. Maybe he'd knocked Zac slightly off balance and that was why he leaned even closer to her. It was no excuse, though, was it?

You really shouldn't kiss somebody you'd only just met. Somebody who you were probably going to be working with on an almost daily basis.

Summer couldn't deny that she'd been thinking about kissing him. Couldn't deny that sudden attraction. Had it been contagious?

Who actually moved first or was it just the result of that movement on top of already sitting so close?

Not that it mattered. Nothing seemed to matter for the brief blink of time that Zac's lips touched her own. The touch was so electric that she jerked back instinctively. She'd never felt *anything* like that...

Flint's deep bark couldn't be ignored. Jay was walking towards them. The random sound of a frog croaking from her beach bag was another alert. She had a text message on her phone.

Real life was demanding her attention but, for a crazy moment, Summer wanted it to just go away. She wanted to sit on the sand as the sun set.

She wanted to kiss Zac again.

Properly, this time...

'So...' Zac had noticed Flint's enthusiastic greeting and must have guessed that it was Jay coming to collect the board. 'How 'bout that drink?'

Summer was also getting to her feet. She'd scooped up her bag and was checking her phone. It could be an emergency call-out.

Except it wasn't. It was a text from Kate.

It's driving me nuts trying to guess. You don't mean Zac M, do you? OMG. If it is, stay AWAY.

Somehow Summer managed a friendly introduction between Jay and her new work colleague despite the chaos in the back of her mind as memories forced themselves to the surface.

Driving Kate up to Auckland late that night because Shelley had been hospitalised after an attempted suicide. Listening to the hysterical account of the man she'd been abandoned by. The father of her baby. The monster who'd tried to push her down a staircase when he'd learned that she was pregnant...

So many buttons could be pushed by memories that could never be erased.

And she'd actually wanted to *kiss* him again?

'I'll give you a hand closing up,' she heard herself saying to Jay as he picked up her board. She barely glanced over her shoulder. 'See you later, Zac.'

CHAPTER THREE

HE HAD NO one to blame other than himself.

How stupid had he been?

Even now, a good twenty hours after the incident, the realisation that he'd *kissed* Summer Pearson was enough to make him cringe inwardly. Or maybe it was an echo of the flinch his current patient had just made.

'Sorry, mate. It's just the local going in. It's a deep wound.'

'Tell me about it. As if it wasn't bad enough getting bitten by the damn dog, I had to rip half my leg open on the barbed wire fence getting away from it. Bled like a stuck pig, I did.'

'I'll bet.' Zac reached for the next syringe of local that Mandy had drawn up for him. 'Almost there. We can start stitching you up in a minute.'

'You won't feel a thing,' Mandy assured him. 'You've got the best doctor in the house.'

'At least he's a bloke. D'you know, there were two *girls* on the ambulance that came to get me?'

'Hadn't you heard, Mr Sanders?' Mandy's tone was amused. 'Girls can do anything these days. Can't we, Zac?'

'Absolutely. I'd say you were a lucky man, Mr Sanders. Can you pass me the saline flush, please, Mandy? I'd like to give this a good clean-out before we start putting things back together.'

He took his time flushing out the deep laceration. He'd do the deep muscle suturing here but he had every intention of handing over to Mandy to finish the task. It might do his patient good to realise that girls could be trusted to do all sorts of things these days.

Like fly around in helicopters and save people's lives. Not that he'd seen Summer do anything that required a high level of skill yesterday but he was quite confident that she had the capability to impress him. He was looking forward to a job that would challenge them both.

At least, he *had* been looking forward to it.

What had he been thinking on the beach yesterday evening? That because she seemed to be thawing towards him he'd make a move and ensure that she actually had a good reason to hate working with him?

Idiot...

Except it hadn't been like that, had it?

Zac reached for the curved needle with the length of absorbable suture material attached. He touched the base of the wound at one side.

'Can you feel that?'

'Nope.'

'Okay. Let me know if you do feel anything.'

'Sure will.'

Zac inserted the needle at the base of the wound and then brought it out halfway up the other side. Pulling it through, he inserted it in the opposite side at the same level and then pulled it through at the base again. This meant he could tie it at the bottom and bury the knots to reduce tissue traction, which would give a better cosmetic result.

His patient was happy to lie back on his pillow,

his hands behind his head, smiling at Mandy, who was happy to keep him distracted while Zac focused on his task.

'What sort of dog was it, Mr Sanders?'

'No idea. Horrible big black thing. Bit of Rottweiler in it, I reckon, judging by the size of those teeth.'

Zac tried to tune out from the chat. Tried not to think about big black dogs. But the suturing was a skill that was automatic and it left his mind free to circle back yet again to how things had gone so bottom-up on the beach.

He'd been enjoying himself. Taking pleasure in sitting beside an attractive young woman, sharing his favourite place with someone who loved it as much as he did. Feeling as if he was making real progress in forging a new professional relationship because of the way Summer had been telling him about part of her personal life. Loving the idea of such a faithful bond between owner and dog that a bit of ocean wasn't about to separate them.

And suddenly something had changed dramatically. He'd been shoved sideways by the dog and Summer had been looking at him and it felt as if he was seeing who she really was for the first time and he'd liked what he was seeing.

Really liked it.

But he didn't go around kissing women just because he found them attractive. No way. He would never force himself on a woman, either. *Ever.* Being made to feel as if he had done that stirred feelings that were a lot less than pleasant.

The needle slid in and out of flesh smoothly and the wound was closing nicely but Zac wasn't feeling the satisfaction of a job being done well. He was in the same emotional place he'd been left in last night, when Summer had virtually dismissed him and walked away without a backward glance.

If it wasn't beyond the realm of something remotely believable, he might have decided that it was Summer who'd initiated that kiss but the way she'd jerked back in horror had made it very clear that hadn't been the case.

He felt as if he'd been duped. Manipulated in

some incomprehensible way. Pulled closer and then slapped down. Treated unfairly.

The final knot of the deep sutures was pulled very tight. The snip of the scissors a satisfying end note.

Okay…he was angry.

He needed to put it aside properly before it had any chance of affecting his work. At least he was in the emergency department today. He was due for another shift on the helicopter tomorrow but maybe he'd find time to ring the base manager later and ask if he could juggle shifts.

With a bit of luck, he could find another crew to work with, without having to tell anybody why he couldn't work with Summer again.

The call-out had been more than welcome.

'Big MVA up north.' Her crew partner today was Dan. 'You ready to rock and roll, Summer?'

'Bring it on.'

It was very unfortunate for the people in the vehicles that had collided head-on at high speed on an open road, but Summer had been suffering from cabin fever for several hours by now. She needed action. Enough action to silence the internal conflict that seemed to be increasingly loud.

The usual distractions that a quiet spell provided hadn't worked. She should have made the most of the time to catch up on journal articles or do some work on the research project she had going but, instead, she'd paced around. Checking kits and rearranging stock. Cleaning things, for heaven's sake.

A bit like the way she'd acted when she'd got home last night and couldn't settle to cook or eat any dinner because she kept going over and over what had happened on the beach.

Trying to persuade herself that that kiss had been all Zac's idea. That she hadn't felt what she had when his lips had touched hers.

She was still experiencing those mental circles today and, if anything, they were even more confusing, thanks to that conversation she'd had with Kate late in the evening.

Of course he's charming. Why do you think Shelley fell for him so hard?

But it was more than a surface charm designed to lure women into his bed on a temporary basis.

Zac cared. About elderly patients. About small boys who might have been washed off a rock and drowned.

Small boys. Children. Presumably babies. And if he cared about other people's children, it just didn't fit that he'd abandoned his own. The story was getting old now. Maybe she hadn't remembered the details so well. Kate had been happy to remind her.

Yes...of course he knew Shelley was pregnant. That was why he tried to push her down the stairs.

So why hadn't Shelley pressed charges or demanded paternal support?

She was too scared to have anything more to do with him. And she planned to terminate the pregnancy, remember? Only, in the end, she didn't...

And Zac had been on the other side of the world by then. And Shelley had had one health issue after another. Always at the doctor's or turning up at the Hamilton emergency department Kate still worked in. Things hadn't changed much, either—except now it was her son who always seemed to be sick or getting injured. The whole family had to focus on supporting Shelley and little Felix and sometimes it was a burden.

'Are you going to tell Shelley?' she finally had to ask.

God, I don't know...I might have a chat to her psychiatrist about it. The new meds seem to be working finally, at the moment. It might be bad news to throw a spanner in the works...

It had been Summer who'd thrown the spanner. Not only at Kate but, potentially, at Zac, too. What if Shelley was told? If she took legal action of some kind and demanded a paternity test and back payment of parental support? Or, worse—if she went public with accusations of physical abuse? It could ruin the career Zac was clearly so passionate about. She would not only be responsible for things hitting the fan but she would be stuck in the middle having to work with him.

Why hadn't she just kept her mouth shut? It wasn't as if she saw Kate much these days and she hadn't seen Shelley since that night at the hospital.

But—if it was true—didn't he deserve to face the consequences?

That was the problem in a nutshell, wasn't it?

If it was true. She had no reason to believe it wasn't.

Except what her gut was telling her.

Thank goodness she could stop thinking about it for a while now. She had a job to focus on. A huge job. She could see the traffic banked up in both directions below them now. A cluster of emergency vehicles. She'd heard the updates on the victims. One patient was dead on scene. Another two were still trapped and one of them had a potential spinal injury. The other was having increasing difficulty breathing.

'He was initially responsive to voice,' the paramedic on scene told Summer. 'But he's become unresponsive, with increasing respiratory distress. We've got a wide bore IV in and oxygen on.'

'The passenger?'

'She's not complaining of any pain but she can't move her legs and they're not trapped. She's got a cervical collar on and someone holding her head still while they've been cutting the roof off.'

'And the van driver's status zero?'

'Yes. He was dead by the time we arrived, which was...' the paramedic checked his watch '...twenty-two minutes ago.'

The next few minutes were spent on a rapid assessment of the driver, who was the most critically injured. Summer took note of the jagged metal and other hazards as she went to lean into the car's interior.

'Any undeployed airbags?' Summer had to raise her voice to be heard over the pneumatic cutting gear the fire service were still using to open the badly crushed car.

'No.'

'Is the car stable?'

'Yes. We can roll the dash as soon as you're

ready and then you can get him out. Passenger should be clear for extrication now.'

'Dan, can you coordinate that? I might need you in a minute, though. I'm going to intubate and get another IV in before we move the driver.'

He was already in a bad way and she knew to expect a clinical deterioration as soon as they moved him, even when it was to an area where it would be easier to work. Due to his level of unconsciousness, she didn't need any drugs to help her insert the tube to keep his airway safe. By the time she'd ensured adequate ventilation and got both high flow oxygen and some intravenous fluids running, Dan and his team had extricated the passenger and had her safely immobilised and ready for a slow road trip to the nearest hospital by ambulance.

Summer coordinated the fire crew to help lift the driver from the wreckage and get him onto the helicopter stretcher but she wasn't ready to take off yet. She crouched down at the foot of the stretcher so that she could see his exposed chest at eye level.

'Flail chest,' she told Dan. 'Look at that asymmetrical movement.'

'Here's his driver's licence.' A police officer handed it to Dan. 'His name's Brian Tripp. He's forty-three.'

They already had that information from his wife. There was paperwork the paramedics on scene first had completed. Summer had more important things to deal with. She could hear more clearly with her stethoscope now and she wasn't happy with what she could hear.

'I'm going to do a bilateral chest decompression before we fly,' she decided. 'Can you get the ECG monitor on, Dan? And start fluid resus.'

The only procedure Summer had to deal with a build-up of air in the chest that was preventing the lungs from expanding properly was to insert a needle. It was a temporary measure and it didn't help a lung to re-expand. It also didn't help a build-up of blood instead of air.

And that was the moment—in the midst of dealing with something that was taking her entire focus—that she thought about Zac again.

If only he'd been on board today instead of yesterday. He could have performed a much more useful procedure by actually opening the chest cavity. Not to put a drainage tube in, because that would take too much time, but it was the same procedure and left an opening that would be of far more benefit than the tiny hole a needle could make.

One that could—and did—get blocked when they were in the air only minutes later, even though Monty was keeping them flying low to avoid any pressure changes that could exacerbate the problem.

It was touch and go to keep her patient alive until they reached Auckland General and Summer was virtually running to keep up with the stretcher as they headed for Resus in the ground floor emergency department.

Who knew that Zac Mitchell would be leading the team waiting for them? The wave of relief was odd, given that she had yet to see how this doctor performed under pressure, but there was no denying it was there. Instinct again?

Was it Zac's expression as he caught her gaze? Focused. Intelligent. Ready for whatever she was about to tell him. Not that there was any time for information about what they'd found on scene—like the amount of cabin intrusion that had advertised a potentially serious chest injury. Even the name and age of their patient would have to wait.

'Tension pneumothorax,' she told Zac succinctly. 'Came on en route. He went into respiratory arrest as we landed.'

Within seconds, Zac was performing the exact procedure she had wished he'd been there to perform on scene. And he was doing it with a calm efficiency that—along with the evidence that her patient was breathing for himself again—made Summer even more relieved.

Her instincts about his skill level had not been wrong.

She wanted to stay and watch the resuscitation and assessment that would, hopefully, result in a trip to Theatre to have the major injuries dealt with but another call took her and Dan away with barely enough time to restock their gear.

This was a winch job to collect a mountain biker with a dislocated shoulder who was on a track with difficult access. A road crew were there to take over the care and transport of the patient so there was no return trip to hospital that would have given Summer the chance to find out what had happened to Brian.

She would have been happy to wait until tomorrow. Zac was due to fly with them again and they could have discussed the case. But the base manager, Graham, caught her when she was getting changed at the end of her shift.

'What did you do to Zac yesterday?'

'What do you mean?'

'I had a call. He didn't come out and say it directly but he seems to think it might be better to be attached to a different shift. I told him there weren't any other slots and he said that was fine but...'

Monty was in the locker room at the same time. 'Summer doesn't like him.'

Graham gave her an odd look. 'What's not to like? He's got to be one of the best we've been lucky enough to have on board. What did you say to him?'

'I didn't say anything.'

'You didn't exactly roll out the welcome mat, Summer.' But Monty was smiling. 'And it's not like you to be shy.'

'It's got nothing to do with that.'

'What has it got to do with, then?' Both men were looking at her curiously.

What could she say?

That she knew things about Zac that they didn't know? She'd already caused disruption in other people's lives by telling Kate that he was back in town. How much more trouble would she cause by telling her colleagues? Word would get around in no time flat. She'd never been a troublemaker. Or a gossip, come to that. And it wasn't really any of her business, was it?

Or could she say that she'd met him on the beach last evening and ended up kissing him? That he was possibly so appalled at how unprofessional she'd been that he couldn't see himself being able to work with her again?

Things were getting seriously out of control, here.

'It's nothing,' she snapped. 'Leave it with me. I'll sort it.'

The excuse of getting an update on a major case was a good enough reason to pop into the emergency department on her way home.

Normally, it would be something to look forward to. A professional interaction and discussion that could well be of benefit in her management of similar cases in the future.

But what really needed discussing had nothing to do with her patient from the car accident. It was at the other end of the spectrum of professional versus personal. It felt like a minefield and it was one that had been created because she knew too much.

Or maybe not enough?

Summer felt ridiculously nervous as she scanned the department looking for Zac. He was at the triage desk, looking over Mandy's shoulder at something on a computer screen. When he glanced up and spotted Summer, he smiled politely.

She sucked in a breath. 'You got a minute?'

She looked different.

Maybe it was the clothes. He'd seen her in her flight suit and he'd seen her virtually in her underwear, given what that bikini had covered.

Even now, as he ushered her into his office, the memory gave him a twinge of appreciation that could easily turn into something inappropriate. Something to be avoided at all costs, given the way she had dismissed him so rudely on the beach last night.

It was easy enough to reconnect with the anger at being unfairly treated that was still simmering. Anger that had only received some new fuel by the demonstration of how Summer could blow hot and cold with no obvious encouragement.

He'd already been cool on greeting her. Hadn't said a thing, in fact. He'd just tilted his head with a raised eyebrow in response to her request and excused himself to Mandy before leading the way to his office. He'd seen the surprise in Mandy's expression that he was taking Summer somewhere private to talk. He was a bit surprised himself because there was no reason not to have a professional discussion in front of others and he suspected Summer had come in to follow up on that serious chest injury she'd brought in earlier today.

Except that she looked different. Nervous, almost?

Nah…that seemed unlikely.

Easier to focus on what she was wearing. Leather pants and a tight little jacket.

'You ride a bike?'

'Yeah… It's a requirement for employment on the choppers that you can get to base fast. Even a traffic snarl on the bridge is negotiable with a bike.'

'I know. I ride one myself. A Ducati.'

The quick smile was appreciative. 'Me, too. Can't beat a Ducati.'

'No.' His tone was cool again. Zac wasn't ready

for another compass shift between hot and cold. It was too confusing.

Her smile faded instantly. She looked away. 'I won't take up too much of your time,' she said. 'I just came in to...to apologise, I guess...'

Whoa...this was unexpected. And welcome? Was she going to apologise for making him feel so unwelcome on shift yesterday?

She certainly looked uncomfortable. Zac perched on the corner of his desk but Summer ignored the available chair. She walked over to the bookshelf and looked as if she was trying to read the dates on the thin spines of the entire shelf of *Emergency Medicine Journal*s.

'What happened last night was extremely unprofessional.' Her voice was tight. 'I just wanted to reassure you that it would never happen again.'

She was talking about the kiss rather than her treatment of him as a team member but this was a good start.

Better than good. So why did he have that dull, heavy sensation in his gut that felt remarkably like disappointment?

'And?'

Her head turned swiftly. Her jaw dropped a little. 'And…and I hope you won't let it influence you working on HEMS. Everybody's saying that we're very lucky to have you.'

'Everybody except you.'

Good grief…why couldn't he just accept her apology gracefully? They could shake hands and agree to make a fresh start in their new working relationship, which could solve the issue in the long run.

Because it would be shoving the issue under the carpet, that was why. Yes, they could probably find a way of working together but he'd never know *why* he'd made such a bad first impression.

Summer had bright spots of colour on her cheeks and her eyes were wide and uncertain. Almost…*fearful?* What the hell was going on here?

Zac stood up. He knew it was a bad idea the moment he did it because he was now towering over Summer. Intimidating her. To give her credit, however, he could see the way she straightened. Tilted her chin so that she could meet his gaze without flinching.

'What is it you don't like about me so much, Summer? You don't even *know* me.'

'I know *of* you.' There was a sharp note in her voice. A note that said she was less than impressed with what she knew. Disgusted, even?

Zac's breath came out in a huff of disbelief. 'You amaze me,' he said slowly. 'And I don't mean that as a compliment.'

Anger flashed across her features. 'I grew up in Hamilton,' she snapped. 'I had a road job there as an intensive care paramedic. One of my oldest friends worked as a nurse in the emergency department. Kate, her name is. Kate Jones.'

'How nice for you.' Zac shook his head. 'I have no idea where this is going. Or who Kate Jones is. Or what relevance Hamilton has.'

'Kate has a younger sister who's also a nurse. Shelley Jones. Shelley used to work right here, in Auckland General's emergency department.'

Zac knew he was glaring at her. His eyes were still narrowed as something clicked into place.

'I remember her.' He could feel his mouth twisting into the kind of shape that came when you tasted something very unpleasant. 'She was a bit of a nuisance, in fact.'

'I'll bet she was.' Ice dripped from Summer's clipped words. 'I hope you don't have that kind of *nuisance* in your life too often.'

'What *are* you talking about?'

Her tone was sarcastic now. 'I guess getting girls pregnant could be seen as a bit of a nuisance.'

'*What?*' Time seemed to stop. Alarms sounded. He'd heard of men having their lives destroyed by false accusations of something like sexual abuse. His word against hers and the guy was always guilty until proved innocent. Sometimes it didn't make that much difference when the truth finally came out. Mud always stuck.

But...*pregnancy*?

'I never even went out with Shelley.' The words came out slowly. Cloaked in utter disbelief. 'The nuisance was that she had a fairly obvious crush on me. Kept bringing in gifts, like cakes or flowers. Leaving notes on my locker. Turning up in my street, even.' His anger was surfacing. 'If a guy did that to a girl, he'd be had up for stalking. She was a head case but everybody thought it was a joke.' He pushed stiff fingers through his hair. 'She was pregnant? She *told* people that *I* was the father?'

Shock like this couldn't be feigned.

Summer's mouth had gone completely dry. No wonder she'd been having so much trouble fighting her instincts. Zac was telling the truth.

'Only me and Kate.' She tried to swallow. Tried—and failed—to meet his gaze. 'It was when we had to go and see her when she got admitted to psyche after a suicide attempt.'

And she hadn't thought to query how stable Shelley was at that point? To even wonder if her story was accurate?

'Oh, this just gets better and better,' Zac snapped. 'Don't tell me—I was somehow responsible for this as well?'

He might as well know the worst. Would she want to, if she was in his position?

It was hard to get the words out, though. She really, really didn't want to make this any worse for him. She was only the messenger but a part of her knew she deserved to be shot. She'd treated him unfairly. Appallingly unfairly.

'She…um…told us you'd tried to push her down a flight of stairs. After…um…she'd told you about the baby.'

'And where was I when this was going on?'

'I think you'd left for London the day before.'

'How convenient.' Zac was pacing. Two steps in one direction and then an about-face for two steps back as if he felt the desperate need to go somewhere. Anywhere but here. He shoved his fingers through his hair, making the dark waves stand up in a tousled mess.

Then he stopped still and turned slowly to stare at Summer.

'And you *believed* her?'

She'd never felt so small. Strangely, he didn't look angry at the moment, although that would undoubtedly resurface. She could see disbelief. Deep disappointment. Anguish, even…

'As you said…I didn't know you. I'd never met you. All I knew was your name.'

'You met me yesterday.' Yes. There was anger there as well and the words were accusing. 'And you still believed it.'

Summer bit her bottom lip. Would it help to tell him how she'd had doubts from the first instant she'd set eyes on him? How she'd had to fight the feeling of being drawn closer? Of a connection that would have been exciting in any other circumstances? Of a confusion that had ultimately ended in wanting that kiss?

No. She had no excuses. For any of it. She closed her eyes.

'I'm sorry.'

'So am I.'

There was silence for a long moment. A heavy—*where do we go from here?*—kind of silence that she had no idea how to breach.

And then Zac sighed. He perched himself on

the corner of his desk again. Summer risked a glance but he was staring at the floor.

'I guess it's better that I know about it,' he said finally. 'At least I'll be prepared for when she turns up in the department again.'

'She gave up nursing. She's had a struggle with her…um…mental health issues.'

Zac snorted.

'I haven't seen her since she was admitted that time. I don't even see Kate much since I left Hamilton. Nobody else needs to know about this, Zac. I'm sorry I knew. Or thought I knew. I wish she'd never mentioned your name.'

'I'm sure you're not the only person she's "mentioned" it to. It's probably on some record somewhere. Like a birth certificate? Oh, my God…' It was clearly sinking home even deeper. 'She did *have* the baby?'

Summer nodded. Her cheeks were burning. 'She told us she was going to have a termination but she didn't. She went down south to stay with friends and apparently came back with the baby to land on her parents' doorstep, asking for help. It was a boy. Felix. He'd be about two and a half now.'

'So I'm probably on some social security list, somewhere. As a father who's failed to provide child support.'

Summer couldn't answer that.

'I hope I am,' Zac said surprisingly. 'A quick DNA test will sort that out.' His huff was incredulous. 'I never even kissed her.'

He caught her gaze with those words. She completely believed that he'd never kissed Shelley.

But he had kissed her. And, for a heartbeat, that was all Summer could think of. That jolt of sensation that had been like some kind of electrical shock.

'It wasn't an immaculate conception,' Zac said dryly. 'It was an entirely imaginary one. Why, in God's name, would anybody *do* something like that?'

'I don't know,' Summer whispered.

Except—maybe—deep down, she did know. Zac Mitchell was the embodiment of a fantasy boyfriend. The ultimate husband and father for your baby. Something to dream about that was never likely to happen for real.

If you were desperate enough and maybe *sick* enough then, yes…she could imagine how somebody would do something like that.

But to make it so completely believable? That was what she really couldn't understand. Her instincts hadn't warned her about anything remotely off, that night. She'd still believed it after talking to Kate last night. Until she'd heard and seen the irrefutable truth in Zac's voice and body language.

'I'll tell Kate,' she offered. 'She can confront Shelley and get the truth out of her. She owes you one hell of an apology. We *all* owe you that.'

But Zac shook his head. 'I'd rather not rake it up any further. Not unless I have to. I'd rather move on and do what I came back here to do. Focus on my career and combine my ED work with as much time as possible in HEMS.'

'But you'd rather work with another shift?' Summer was trying to find what it was on the floor that had caught Zac's attention earlier. 'I could talk to Graham.'

'He said there weren't any other slots available.'

'I'm sure something could be juggled. A team has to be tight. It just doesn't work if there's a...a personality clash or something.'

Another silence fell. Summer finally had to look up and meet Zac's gaze. An unreadable gaze but the intensity was unmistakable.

'But we don't, do we?'

'Don't what?'

'Have a personality clash.'

She couldn't look away. She was being sucked in again. Like the way she had been when she'd been sitting beside him on the paddleboard last night. In that moment before she'd kissed him.

'No...'

'So why don't we just try and make a fresh start and see how it goes?'

Hope was something wonderful. A close cousin of both relief and excitement.

'You'd be okay with that?'

'If you are.'

It felt like the first time she was smiling at Zac. The first time it was a truly genuine smile, anyway.

Nothing else needed to be said because Zac smiled back.

The moment seemed to hang in time. And then it became just a little bit awkward. As though more was being communicated than either of them were ready for.

Zac cleared his throat. 'Do you want to hear about the surgery on that tension pneumothorax guy you brought in?'

'Oh…' Summer's nod was probably a shade too enthusiastic. 'Yes, please…'

'Come with me. I'll show you the scans first. Man, that chest was a mess. I'm impressed that you got him here alive.'

Summer followed Zac out of his office. Their fresh start seemed to be happening now.

How good was that?

CHAPTER FOUR

ZAC'S BIKE WAS BIG, black and sleek.

It made Summer's smaller red model look feminine but the assumption would be deceptive. Only a certain kind of woman rode a machine like that.

Confident, feisty kind of women. And when they were wrapped up in a small package that could easily be seen as 'cute', it was a very intriguing mix. She must have arrived for work only seconds before he'd pulled into the rescue helicopter's base because she was standing beside her bike, pulling off her helmet. A glove came off next and the flattened spikes of her hair were fluffed up with a quick, spread finger comb-through—the feminine gesture at odds with the stance. With her feet apart and her helmet cradled under one arm making it look as if she had the hand on her hip, Summer Pearson looked ready to take on the world.

And she was watching him as he killed his engine and got off his own bike. Her gaze was... cautious?

Of course it was. This was the first time they were on base together after that extraordinary conversation in his office. And, yes, they'd agreed to make a fresh start and see how it went but how was that going to work, exactly? He'd had time to try and think it through but, if anything, he was finding it all increasingly disturbing.

Part of Zac—the angry part—wanted nothing more than to seek Shelley out and demand a retraction of accusations that were unbelievably malicious, but the voice of reason was warning him not to do anything without thinking it through very carefully. Yes, he could prove the child wasn't his but there were those appalling accusations of violence against a woman and that would be her word against his.

The people who knew him would never believe it but he didn't even want them to have to *think* about it. Imagine how upset his grandmother would be. It was something they never talked about these days—the way he'd seen his mother treated by the man who'd come into their lives when he'd been old enough to start remembering. Old enough to think that it was his fault and he needed to do something to defuse the tension that always ended with his mum bruised and crying.

Summer was taking his word for his innocence in regard to what she'd thought she knew about him. That was disturbing, too. Zac felt as though he still needed to prove himself in some way and he should never have had to feel like that.

There was a smudge of resentment in his mood and it was unfamiliar and unwelcome.

So maybe his gaze was just as cautious but they'd agreed to try a fresh start and Zac always kept his end of a bargain.

'Is that a Monster?'

'Yeah. A six five nine.' There was a definite note of relief in Summer's voice at the choice of an impersonal topic of conversation. A softening of her body language as she turned to look at *his* bike. 'About half the cc rating of yours, I expect.'

'Bet you'd still keep up. Maybe we should go for a ride one day.' The invitation was deliberately casual. A little forced, even? They were both trying to create a new base for a working relationship but the ice was potentially a little thin and they were both treading carefully.

'Sure. I like stretching out on the open road when I get a chance.'

They walked side by side into the building and Zac could feel some of the tension ease. Maybe it was more important than he cared to admit that he could prove himself to Summer. That it wasn't just his word she needed to trust but that she would get to know him well enough to understand just how impossible it would be for him to act in the way she'd believed he had acted. If he could convince someone who had believed the worst, he wouldn't need to fear any repercussions if the story became public.

Thinking about a place they could head to on a bike ride—like a beautiful beach, maybe—was premature, however. It was quite possible that Summer was just being polite, the way she was making it about the ride rather than his company. She'd had time to think things through in the last couple of days, too. Time to talk to her friend Kate again, perhaps. She might have changed her mind about taking his word for his innocence but was giving him the benefit of some doubt in the meantime. It wasn't just that she needed to trust him—he needed to trust her, as well. And right now his trust in women was justifiably fragile.

It certainly wouldn't be helpful to mention a beach. To remind her of what had happened the last time they'd been sitting on a beach together. That had been even more premature. Unbelievably so, in fact. Zac still couldn't understand quite how that kiss had happened. Something else they needed to put behind them so they could move on with a more professional relationship? As far as building a base for their new working relationship, this was a minefield. Casual conversation was called for. The kind any new colleagues might have.

'You got four wheels as well as two?'

'No.' Summer gave him a quizzical glance. 'Why would I?'

'Doesn't it make things tricky when you want to take your dog somewhere with you?'

'We run.'

'*Everywhere?*'

Summer popped the studs on her jacket and started peeling it off. 'Everywhere we need to go, usually. If I have to take Flint to the vet or something, I'll get a friend to give us a ride. If I'm not at work or at home, we're generally at the beach. He gets a run there every day.'

'Guess I'll get to meet him again, then. I try and run on Takapuna beach every day.'

'Takapuna's our paddleboard beach. I have to use one of Jay's because it would be a bit tricky to carry one on a bike. If it's just a run or a swim we're after, we've got half a dozen beaches and bays to choose from. Or we can just jump over-board.'

'Sorry?' Zac was folding up his leather jacket. He couldn't see Summer because she was behind the open door of her locker now. He was sure he hadn't heard her correctly but then her face popped out and she was smiling. Really smiling. A real smile—like the one she'd given him in his office the other day, when they'd agreed to start again. A smile that could light up the darkest place.

'We live on a boat.'

'Oh...' Zac was lost for words. Just when he thought he was getting a handle on his new colleague, the rug got pulled out from beneath his feet. It wasn't just the unusual place to call home. That smile was doing something strange to his gut. It was more than relief that things seemed to be on a better footing. More, even, than the way it reminded him of what her lips had felt like for that brief instant. Maybe it was the impish quality—the hint of sheer *joie de vivre*—that made it impossible not to smile back.

'What sort of boat?'

'An old yacht. A thirty-foot Catalina. Her name's *Mermaid*. I'm not sure she'd be seaworthy to take out but I've been renting her to live in ever since I came up to Auckland. It's the only home Flint's ever known. He'd be a sad dog if he couldn't see the sea.'

'What does he do when you're at work?'

'Guards the boat. Or sleeps on the jetty. Everybody at the marina knows him. He's never wandered. Never needs a lead. He only wears a collar to hang his registration tag on and make him legal.'

Summer was pulling her flight suit on over her shorts and T-shirt. Her curves were disappearing beneath the shapeless garment and maybe that was just as well.

Zac was beginning to realise what an extraordinary woman Summer was. With the absence of the hostility with which they'd started working together, he was getting far more of a glimpse of what she was like. Fiercely independent, judging by her choice of lifestyle. Open-minded, maybe, given that she was prepared to take his word over that of a long-term friend. The relationship she had with her dog suggested a mutual loyalty and—a bit like her pet—maybe she was a free spirit who chose exactly where she wanted to be and who she wanted to be with. You couldn't lead Summer anywhere she didn't want to go.

But how privileged would you be if she chose to go with you?

Hang on a minute...she'd said 'we' live on a boat. He'd assumed she was talking about herself and her dog but what if there was another component to that 'we'?

That might go even further than both the misinformation on his past and prematurity in having made that kiss so shocking for her. No wonder this all felt so complicated.

Zac took a mental step backwards. Yep. He really did need to tread a little more carefully. There was still a lot more he needed to learn about Summer.

A trip to one of the inhabited islands right out in the Hauraki Gulf was always a bit of a treat. The longer flying time provided an opportunity to enjoy the spectacular views below. The harbour was busy, with ferries and yachts out enjoying the afternoon breeze. There was even a sleek cruise ship in the channel between Rangitoto Island and Takapuna beach.

'Tough day at the office.'

Summer laughed. 'You said it, Monty. And— even better—we're off to deliver a baby.'

'Might have arrived by the time we get there,' Zac warned. 'How far apart did she say her contractions were?'

'Five minutes. And Comms said she sounded a bit distressed.'

'I'm not surprised. It's an isolated place to give birth if something goes wrong.'

'She might be a bit earlier than full-term. It's usual practice for women to go to the mainland for delivery.' Summer was still enjoying the view. 'That's Tiritiri Matangi island. You ever been there?'

'No. Love lighthouses, though. It's a bird sanctuary, isn't it?'

'Yes. It's well worth a visit.' Summer took a breath, about to say something more, but then she closed her mouth.

Had she been about to suggest that they took a ride up to Gulf Harbour on their bikes the next time they had a day off at the same time? And then take the ferry and walk around the island, seeing things like the feeding stations that attracted hundreds of bellbirds and tuis?

Yep. Even now, the idea of spending a day like that with Zac was extremely appealing but he might have just been being polite, suggesting that they had a ride together. After all, it was a working relationship they'd agreed to make a fresh start on, not a personal one.

Wasn't it?

They were met at the landing site by a man called Kev, who was in charge of Civil Defence and the volunteer fire brigade for the small community. A retired fisherman with an impressive white beard, Kev had an ancient jeep to provide transport. The local nurse was unavailable to assist because she'd taken the ferry to the mainland to go shopping.

'Janine? Yep. I know where she lives. Haven't

seen her for a while but she likes to keep to herself. She's sick?'

'In labour, apparently.'

'She's having a *baby*?'

Summer caught Zac's glance as he lifted the Thomas pack of gear into the back of the jeep. This was odd. In such a small community, surely a full-term pregnancy wouldn't go unnoticed?

Kev started the engine. It coughed and died so he tried again. This time it caught but he was shaking his head.

'A baby…well…how 'bout that?'

Summer climbed into the vehicle. 'You didn't know she was pregnant?'

Kev grinned. 'She's a big girl, is Janine. Can't say I noticed last time either, mind you.' He clicked his tongue. 'That was a sad business…'

'Oh? In what way?' Under normal circumstances, it might not be ethical to be discussing a patient with someone who wasn't a family member but the comment was ringing alarm bells. If the last birth had caused major problems, they needed to know about it.

'She did all the right things. Went to the big hospital in Whangerei to have the bub. Dunno what happened exactly, but it didn't come home. Janine was in bits. Broke her and Ev up in the end. He lives over on the mainland now but she goes off on the ferry to visit him sometimes so... Guess they must have decided to try again. She shouldn't be having it here, though, should she? Crumbs...what if something goes wrong again?'

'That's why we're here.' Zac's tone was calm. Reassuring. 'How far is it to her house?'

'It's not a house, exactly. More like a caravan with a bit built on. It's not too far. Up in the bush at the end of this beach coming up.'

'Does she have any family here?'

'Nah.'

'Friends?'

Kev scratched his beard as he brought the jeep to a halt. 'She gets on okay with everybody but, like I said, she keeps to herself pretty much. 'Specially since the trouble. Want me to come in with you?'

Summer caught Zac's gaze. There could be a

reason why Janine had been keeping her pregnancy private.

'How 'bout you wait out here for us, Kev? We'll see what's happening and hopefully you can get us all back to the chopper pretty fast.'

Except that it didn't look as if they'd be moving their patient any time too soon.

Janine was inside the caravan, hanging onto the edge of the built-in table with one hand and clutching her belly with the other. She saw Summer and Zac ease themselves into the cramped space but clearly couldn't say anything in response to their introductions. Her face was contorted with pain.

'Contraction?'

Janine nodded, groaning at the same time.

'How long since the last one?'

Their patient shook her head. 'Dunno,' she gasped.

'Have your waters broken?'

A nod this time.

'We need to check what's happening,' Zac said. 'Would you prefer it if Summer examines you?'

Janine shook her head. 'You're the doctor. I'm...*scared...*'

'Let's get you on your bed.' Summer took Janine's arm to encourage her to move. 'We can help you. It might help us if you can tell us about what happened last time...'

But Janine burst into tears as she climbed onto the narrow bed. She covered her face with her hands. Summer could see the swell of the young woman's belly now that she was lying flat. She helped her bend her knees so that Zac could find out how advanced the labour was.

He was frowning when he looked up a short time later.

'No dilation whatsoever,' he said. 'No cervical softening, even.'

'Really?' Summer placed her hands on Janine's belly. 'Let's see if I can find out how Baby's lying.'

The swollen belly felt firm. And oddly smooth.

'Has Baby been moving?'

'Yes. Lots. Until this morning, anyway...'

Zac was unpacking the portable ultrasound

unit. 'Have you been going over to the mainland for your antenatal checks, Janine?'

'No...' She turned her head away from them. 'I didn't trust the doctors at the hospital. Or the midwives. Not after last time...'

'What happened, love?' Zac paused, the tube of gel in his hands.

'It was all fine until I was in the hospital. They said it was a knot in the cord and it...it stopped the oxygen. I knew something was wrong but they were still telling me to push and I...I...'

'It's okay, Janine.' Summer caught her hand. 'You're having contractions now but you're nowhere near giving birth. We're going to get you to a safe place in plenty of time.'

Zac was pressing the ultrasound probe to Janine's belly, staring at the small screen of the unit. He was frowning again. He shifted the probe and tilted the screen so that Summer could see it. She stared too, totally bewildered.

'We just need some more gear,' Zac said calmly. 'We want to take your blood pressure and things, Janine. Be back in a tick.'

But... Summer stifled the word. They had all
the gear they needed in the pack right beside
them but she recognised the warning glance and
followed Zac into the lean-to built onto the caravan that was a living area with armchairs and a
potbelly stove.

She kept her voice low. 'There's no baby, is
there?'

Zac shook his head.

'But she *looks* pregnant. She's having contractions. She's in *labour.*'

'She *thinks* she's in labour.' Zac spoke just as
quietly. 'This is incredibly rare but I think it's a
case of pseudocyesis.'

'Phantom pregnancy? Good grief...what do we
do?'

'She needs help. When she finds out that she's
not actually pregnant, it's going to be as devas-
tating as losing her first baby. This isn't the time
or place for that to happen.'

'So we go along with it? Transport her, believing that she's still about to give birth? Give her
pain relief for the contractions?'

'What else can we do?'

There was no answer to that. Getting Janine to the specialist psychiatric help she needed was a no-brainer. Making the situation even harder to deal with would have been a stupid option. It took a lot of persuasion to get Janine to agree to transport at all.

'I want to have my baby here. Where it's safe.'

'But it's not safe, Janine. You're too far away from the kind of specialist people and facilities that make it safe. And it's not going to happen for a while. We can't stay but we can't leave you here by yourself either.'

Finally, she agreed. She told Summer where the bag was with all the things she would need for the baby. A glance inside the bag showed some gorgeous hand-knitted booties and hats. A soft pink teddy bear. She was blinking back tears as they helped Janine into the jeep.

'You should've told us, love.' Kev looked worried. 'We were worried about you.'

'I'll be fine, Kev. I'll be back soon. With the baby.'

* * *

It was the strangest case Summer had ever had. She was still thinking about it that evening when she was walking on the beach with Flint.

She'd known there was a good chance of meeting Zac on Takapuna beach. It was easy enough to guess what time he was likely to be having a swim or a run. Maybe that was why she'd chosen this beach, despite not intending to go paddleboarding today. Maybe she wanted the chance to talk about such a puzzling case.

He'd been good to work with today. The fresh start was working well. Maybe there was even a pull to see him again that she wasn't about to admit to.

The excuse that this was where some of Flint's best dog friends came to play was a good cover. And Zac seemed happy enough to sit and chat.

'It was a good day, wasn't it? It's not often you get a "once in a lifetime" case like that.'

'I still can't believe that something imaginary could give rise to actual physical signs.'

'The power of the mind.' Zac nodded. 'It's extraordinary, isn't it?'

'The things she said when I was getting her history down en route. Like the date her periods stopped and the early nausea and breast changes. Feeling the baby starting to move at about sixteen weeks. Everything sounded so normal.'

'She'd been through it before. She knew what to expect.'

'But do you think she could actually feel what she thought was the baby moving?'

'I'm sure she could.'

'And the size and shape of her belly. I couldn't believe it when the ultrasound showed there was no baby.'

'I've read about it. They reckon it's due to changes in the endocrine system. When a woman wants to be pregnant so desperately, it can trick the body into believing it's pregnant, as well as the mind. That triggers the secretion of hormones like oestrogen and prolactin and that will stop periods and cause breast changes and nausea. And the weight gain and belly swelling. So, of course, there's no reason for her to stop believing she's pregnant—it just gets confirmed.'

'But for so many months? To actually go into an imaginary labour?'

'That's really rare. I think that psychiatrist that got called in looked quite excited about the case. He'll probably write it up for a journal article.'

'I just hope he takes good care of Janine. Poor thing.'

'Yeah… You have to feel sorry for her.'

They sat in silence for a while, then, watching Flint do the sniffing thing to greet a small black Spoodle. With an excited yap, the Spoodle ran in a circle and then dipped its head, inviting Flint to chase her. He complied and, a moment later, both dogs were splashing though the shallows at high speed against the backdrop of a pretty sunset over Rangitoto.

Summer felt her smile stretching. Life was good. Shifting her gaze, she found Zac smiling as well and, suddenly, there they were again. Looking at each other like they had been when they'd been sitting on her board the other night.

Only this time it felt different.

Relaxed.

The tension was gone and, just as suddenly, Summer thought she knew why.

'It's been bothering me,' she admitted. 'Why I believed Shelley. My instincts are usually so good about whether people are telling the truth. But it's like Janine, isn't it? What you said about the power of the mind.'

'Not sure I'm following you.'

'If we hadn't had that ultrasound with us, I would have believed Janine was pregnant.'

'She was certainly convincing.'

'So was Shelley.'

'But Shelley *was* pregnant.'

'I'm talking about the other stuff. About you being the father and…' No, she didn't even want to think about the accusations of violence. Zac had been so kind to poor Janine and the compassion in his voice had suggested he felt as sorry for her as others should. He'd made a terrifying situation bearable for Frances the other day. He adored his gran. It would be insulting to even voice something so unbelievable. 'But maybe she was believable because that's what she believed herself.'

Zac grunted. 'She's pretty sick, then.'

'Like Janine.'

'Janine's only hurting herself.'

'We don't know that for sure. There could be collateral damage for others—like her ex-husband? He might be involved enough to believe he's about to have another child.'

'I guess. You could be right. Maybe feeling sorry for Shelley is the best way to go.' Zac's sigh suggested that he didn't want to talk about it any more and that was fair enough.

Flint was shaking water from his coat as the Spoodle took off to rejoin its owner further down the beach. Any moment now and he'd probably come back, all damp and sandy, and she might have to excuse herself to go and finish their walk. Or maybe not. Zac might not want to talk about Shelley any more but he didn't seem annoyed when he spoke again.

'So you have good instincts, then?'

'I've always thought so.'

'Just out of interest—given what you thought you knew—what did those instincts tell you about me the other day?'

That was easy to answer. 'That you couldn't possibly be the monster I'd assumed you were.' She smiled. 'No one but an exceptionally nice person could start talking about his gran the moment he opened his mouth.'

Zac grinned and Summer found herself saying more than she'd intended to say. 'I liked you,' she admitted. 'It felt wrong but I…I *really* liked you.'

Zac was silent for a moment. It looked as if he might be taking a rather slow breath. Then he cleared his throat. 'Just for the record, I really liked you too. I still do.'

Another silence as Summer absorbed his words. Oh, yeah… Life was good.

'And what did those instincts tell you when we were on the beach the other night? When I… kissed you.'

'But *I* kissed *you*.'

'I don't think so.' There was amusement in his

tone. 'At least, that's not the way I remember it.' He caught her gaze. 'You wouldn't have been so shocked if it had been your idea,' he added. 'You jumped like you'd got burned.'

'That was because it felt...weird...'

'Weird?'

'Yeah...' Summer had to break the eye contact. 'Different. Yeah...weird.'

'Hmm.' Another pause and then the query was interested. 'Good weird or bad weird?'

Summer tried to remember that odd jolt. To feel it again. But all that she was aware of was a growing warmth in her belly, spreading into her limbs. A tingly, delicious kind of warmth.

'I think...good weird.'

'But you're not sure?'

'No...' *Oh, my...* That look in Zac's eyes right now. The sheer mischief. The *intent*...

'I'm thinking there's only one way to find out.'

Did he mean what she thought he meant? That he would have to kiss her again?

Had he really thought he'd been the one who'd initiated the kiss the other night?

There could only be one explanation for that. That they'd both been thinking exactly the same thing. At the same time.

And they were doing it again right now. Summer's heart skipped a beat and picked up its pace.

Or maybe not.

'Not here,' Zac said. 'It's way too public.'

The disappointment was fleeting because the prospect of being somewhere more private was infinitely more exciting. Zac was already on his feet, ready to take her to that private place. Summer's heart was still thumping and now her mouth felt a little dry.

Or maybe not.

'Come and meet my gran.'

CHAPTER FIVE

HE'D WANTED TO take her home.

So he could kiss her again. Properly. Last time it had been a kind of accident that didn't count but even the memory of that brief brush of their lips gave him a twist of very powerful desire. And Summer remembered it well enough to think it was different? Weird but good?

She had no idea how good it *could* be…

It would have sounded crass to say that out loud and it could well have scared her off completely so he'd had to come up with another reason to get them away from such a public place.

But introducing her to his grandmother?

Now they were stuck. Flint looked happy enough on the terrace outside and Summer looked happy enough inside. Zac had come back from taking a quick shower and changing his clothes to find her helping his gran put a salad together—to go with the massive salmon fillet that just happened to have been baking in the oven this evening.

Ivy Mitchell had been thrilled to meet Summer.

'So you're the girl who has the dog on the back of the board? I watch you every time, dear. With my telescope.'

'Really?' Summer looked disconcerted. 'I had no idea people were spying on me.'

'Oh, I spy on everybody, darling. I'm ninety-two. Nobody's going to tell me off.'

'I might,' Zac growled. 'You can't go around spying on people, Gravy.'

'I'm not gainfully employed. I sit on my terrace and the telescope's right there. What's a girl supposed to do?'

Summer was laughing. And shaking her head. *'Gravy?'*

Ivy smiled. 'I told Isaac's mum that I didn't want to be called Granny. I wasn't even sixty when he was born, for heaven's sake. Far too young! I said he could call me Ivy, like a real person, but she said I had to be Gran. So it was supposed to be Gran Ivy but it was too hard for him when he was learning to talk so it came out as Gravy. And it stuck.'

'I love it. The only grandmother I had was Nana, which seems terribly ordinary in comparison.'

'Had?'

'She died when I was quite young.'

'What a shame. The older generation is a blessing. Your family must miss that.'

'I don't have any family. My mum died when I was seventeen and my father was already well out of the picture.' Summer's tone was brisk and Zac recognised that it was not a topic open to further discussion. It reminded him of that first day in the chopper when he'd asked whether she had any siblings. The impression that she could offer personal information but he was not allowed to ask had been so strong he still hadn't tested those boundaries. He had boundaries of his own, didn't he? It might be unspoken but there was an agreement between them now that precluded any more discussion of Summer's friend Kate and her sister Shelley. Of the child he'd been accused of fathering.

Not that Ivy was likely to respect such boundaries. Except that this time she did. She opened her mouth but then closed it again, simply handing Summer a jar with a screw lid. 'Throw this dressing on the salad, darling. I make it myself and it's got a lovely garlic punch. So good for you, you know—garlic.'

'It's your secret to a long life, isn't it, Gravy?'

'That—and champagne, of course. Speaking of which, let's refresh our glasses, shall we, Summer? Champagne and salmon—a marriage made in heaven.'

Zac took a pull at the icy glass of lager he held. The view from the upper level of this old house was extraordinary—like a huge painting of a beach scene with the background of the sea and the distinctive volcano shape of Rangitoto Island placed perfectly dead centre. Right now, there were vivid streaks of red in the sky as daylight ended with a spectacular flourish. He had always loved the changing panorama of this living painting. He loved this house. Right now, he loved that a contented dog lay with his nose on his paws guarding the house and its occupants. He could smell good food and he was with the person who meant the most to him in the world—his beloved Gravy.

Could life get any better?

Maybe it could.

He was also with an extraordinary newcomer to his life. The idea of getting to know Summer a great deal better was exciting. Maybe—just maybe—this was the woman who could capture him enough to be the person he had yet to find. The one who could come to mean as much—or possibly even more—than his only family member.

The possibility was as breathtaking as the view.

Zac watched the conspiratorial grin between the two women as they clinked champagne flutes and he had to smile. Kindred spirits? They were certainly getting on very well together. He just hoped that second glass of bubbles wouldn't loosen his grandmother's tongue any further. Bad enough that she'd already admitted spying on Takapuna residents as they enjoyed their beach. How much worse would it be if she started on another favourite theme—that it was high time her grandson found a nice girl and settled down to start making babies?

As if she felt both the gaze and his smile, Summer turned her head and her gaze locked with his. And there was that kick of desire in his gut again. How long would it take them to eat dinner and escape? To find somewhere they could be alone together?

Maybe Summer was telepathic. He could see the way her chest rose as if she was taking a deep breath. The way her eyes darkened, suggesting that her thoughts mirrored his. When the tip of her tongue appeared to wet her lips, he almost uttered a growl of frustration. However long dinner took, it was going to be too long.

If Summer was lucky enough to live until she was in her nineties, she wanted to be exactly like Ivy Mitchell.

A little taller than Summer, Ivy was very slim but it would be an insult to call her frail. She had long silver hair that was wound up into an elegant knot high on the back of her head and her clothing was just as chic, white Capri pants and a dark blue tee shirt with a white embroidered anchor on it. As someone with sea water in her veins, maybe that was why she'd instantly felt at ease with Zac's grandmother.

Unusually at ease. Was it the age gap? Way too much to be a friend or a colleague. Too much, even, to be an age group that invited comparison to her mother, which was a good thing because Ivy's relaxed confidence, that was so like her grandson's, would have made her mother's constant anxiety seem awkward.

Or maybe it was because she had the same warm brown eyes as her gorgeous grandson. Whatever the reason, Summer was enjoying herself and feeling increasingly relaxed, which was ironic because the energy level emanating from Ivy was leaving her feeling rather breathless.

Or maybe that had something to do with the

way Zac was looking at her every time she met his gaze. As if he really liked what he was seeing. As if he couldn't wait to see more.

And eating dinner with these two...

Oh, my...

Watching food going into Zac's mouth and the way he licked the corners of his lips occasionally to catch a drip of salad dressing was doing very strange things to her equilibrium.

This was crazy. She'd only met him last week. Summer Pearson did not go around jumping into bed with men she'd only just met. Especially men she hadn't even been on a date with. But what if time together counted, even if it hadn't been pre-arranged? Sitting on a beach with someone was *almost* like a date, wasn't it?

If Ivy had any idea of where her thoughts kept drifting, she wasn't bothered.

'So you live on a boat? I love that. But isn't it a bit cramped?'

'We manage. You do have to be tidy. And not collect too much junk.'

'We?' Ivy's eyebrows shot up. 'You have a *man* in your life, Summer?'

'Ah...' Summer kept her gaze firmly on the flakes of salmon she was spearing with her fork. 'Only Flint. He has to be tidy, too.'

'Of course he does.' There was a satisfied note in Ivy's voice and Summer looked up to catch the significant look she was giving Zac. There might have been an eyebrow wiggle involved as well.

It was cringe-worthy but then Zac grinned at her and winked and suddenly it was fine.

More than fine.

Summer grinned back. She had just fallen a little bit in love with Zac Mitchell.

'You know, I think I've been a bit of a pelican,' Ivy declared. 'My eyes held more than my belly can. Do you think Flint might be able to finish this for me? Salmon's not bad for dogs, is it?'

'It would be a huge treat for him.'

'Let's bring him inside, then.'

'Oh, I don't think you want to do that. You have no idea how much sand gets trapped in those fluffy paws.'

'Pfft...' Ivy waved her hand. 'What's a bit of sand between friends? I track it in every day myself.'

Summer went to invite Flint inside. Ivy insisted on giving him the salmon off her own plate and Summer shook her head but she was smiling. She had just fallen a little bit in love with Zac's grandmother as well.

'Where does he sleep?' Ivy asked. 'On the boat?'

'Yes. He has his own bed under the cockpit. A double berth, even.'

'Oh... I hope you have a double berth, too...'

Zac's sigh was clearly audible but Ivy winked at Summer. 'Don't mind me,' she said in a stage whisper. 'When you get to my age, you find you can get away with saying almost anything. Sometimes I might get a wee bit carried away.'

Summer smiled. 'I have a very comfortable double bed, Ivy. It's even got an inner-sprung mattress. Speaking of which...' she only had to straighten and look towards the door and Flint was instantly by her side '...I'd better get going. I've got an early start tomorrow.'

Zac pushed his chair back and got to his feet.

The air seemed to have disappeared from the room. What was going to happen now? Would he show her out and kiss her goodnight? How likely was that when Ivy would probably be peeping from a window?

'I'll give you a lift,' he said. 'It's too late to be jogging around the streets.'

'Thanks, but I don't let Flint run after a bike. It's a bit dangerous.'

'Ah...' Zac was almost beside her now. 'Unlike you, I keep four wheels as well as two. I have an SUV with a nice big space for a dog in the back.'

'It'll get full of sand.' But Summer's heart was doing that speeding up thing again. Zac was coming home with her? Would he want to stay for a while?

He was close enough to touch now. She could feel the heat of his body. Or maybe that was heat she was creating herself. A warmth that kicked up several notches as he grinned lazily.

'What's a bit of sand between friends?'

He kissed his grandmother. 'Leave the dishes,' he ordered. 'I'll pop in and do them when I get back.'

Ivy waved them off. 'That's what dishwashers are for. I'll see you tomorrow, Isaac. Don't do anything I wouldn't do, now.'

Zac groaned softly as he closed the door behind them. 'Sorry about that,' he muttered. 'She's incorrigible.'

He'd never been in a yacht that was being used as a permanent home. He'd been sailing, of course. Anyone who grew up beside the sea in Auckland ended up with more than a passing acquaintance with sailing boats.

'She's thirty feet? Feels much bigger inside.'

'It's a great design. Small but perfectly formed.'

Just like Summer?

Zac had to drag his gaze away from her. He'd only just stepped aboard *Mermaid* and, while the invitation to see her home had been freely given, he didn't want to push things too fast, here.

He didn't want to wreck something. Not when so many possibilities were floating so close to touching distance. Mind you, if his gran hadn't scared her off, he was probably in a good space right now.

An astonishing space. There was colour from the warm glow of all the woodwork. A rich blue cushion and padding covered the built-in bench seating around a narrow table and the colour was repeated in a strip of Persian-style carpet down the centre of the floor. The front of the boat's interior was almost closed off by a folding fabric screen but he could see a glimpse of a raised bed with a soft-looking white duvet and fluffy pillows.

Once again, he had to avert his gaze before what he was thinking got printed all over his face.

'Cute sink.'

'It works well, even if it's a single rather than a double. Gives a bit more bench room for cooking. I've got an oven here and even a microwave in this locker, see?'

'Mmm.'

What he liked best about this space was that there wasn't that much room for two people to move around, especially when there was a fairly large dog to avoid, and it was inevitable that they ended up standing extremely close to each other. He had to bend his head a little to admire the microwave oven tucked neatly into its storage space and that put his face extremely close to Summer's as well. Without looking up, he lifted a hand to close the locker and, as he lowered his hand, it felt perfectly natural to brush the spikes of her hair. To let his hand come to rest at the nape of her neck.

To bend his head just a little further so that he could touch her lips with his own. Just a feather-light touch for a heartbeat and then he increased the pressure and touched her lips with his tongue. He felt Summer's gasp as a physical change in her body—the kind of tension that a diver probably had in the moment before she launched herself into space to perform some dramatic series of tumbles and then slice cleanly into the deepest pool. And, as Summer's lips parted beneath his, he knew she had taken that plunge and she was ready to fly.

He had no idea how long they stood there kissing. Zac was aware of nothing more than the delicious taste and the responsiveness of this gorgeous girl. And that the ground was moving slightly beneath his feet. Because they were on a boat? It felt more personal than that. His whole world was gently rocking.

Time had absolutely no relevance because it didn't matter how long it took to explore this wonderful new world. The map was coming into focus and there was no hurry at all to find the right path. The way Summer took the lead to follow that path was possibly the most exciting part about it. She wanted this—as much as he did.

It was her hands that moved first, to disentangle themselves from around his neck to start roaming his body, and that gave him permission to let his own hands move. To shape the delicate bones of her shoulders and trace the length of her spine. To cup the deliciously firm curves of her bottom and the perfection of those surprisingly generous breasts.

It was Summer who took his hand and stopped him undoing another button on the soft shirt she was wearing and, for a moment, Zac had the horrible thought that she was asking him to stop completely. He could, of course, but man, would he need a cold shower when he got home...

It was time to get rid of the audience. A quiet command sent Flint to his bed. Her voice might have wobbled a little but Summer was still holding Zac's hand tightly. She led him to the other end of the boat. Past the screen and up a step to where her bed filled the whole space.

No. It was Zac who was filling this space. The only light was coming from a lamp on the table and the shadows being created gave shedding their clothes a surreal edge—like a scene from an arty movie. And then Zac was kneeling on the bed in front of her and she could flatten her hands against the bare skin of his chest as she raised her face for another kiss and she stopped thinking about the way anything looked. She could only *feel*…

No wonder she'd been shocked by that first ever touch of Zac's lips. She'd never known that arousal could be this intense. That nerve endings could be so sensitised by the lightest touch that the pleasure was almost pain. It was still weird because she'd never felt anything like this before but it was most definitely *good* weird.

Oh, yes…the best weird ever, and she could get used to this.

She wanted to get very, very used to it.

CHAPTER SIX

'TARGET SIGHTED—TWO O'CLOCK.'

The helicopter dipped and shuddered as Monty turned to circle the area. The stiff breeze made the top of the pine forest below sway enough to make an accurate estimation of clearance difficult.

'Not sure I like this,' Monty said. 'Might need to winch you guys in.'

'There's more of a clearing at five o'clock. Where the logging trucks are.'

'It's a fair hike. The guy's having trouble breathing.'

'Winch me down,' Summer said. 'I'll scoop him into the Stokes basket and we can transfer him to the clearing to stabilise him.'

'You happy for Zac to winch you?' Monty's query sounded casual but this was the first time they'd been in a situation like this. In rough weather like this. Yes, Zac was winch trained but Summer would be putting her life in his hands.

She caught Zac's gaze, and even through the muting effect of the visor on his helmet she could see—or maybe sense—the anticipation of her response and, in that instant, a seemingly casual query became so much bigger than being simply about the job they were all doing.

Did she trust Zac?

She *wanted* to. She had never wanted to trust anybody this much. Not with her life because she did that every time she took on a tricky winching job and she was used to putting that kind of trust in her colleagues.

No. This was about trusting a man with her heart and she'd never really done that before. But she *wanted* to. With Zac...

Monty was hovering over the area where the felling accident had occurred. An ambulance was bouncing along the rough track and stopped with a cloud of dust billowing from beneath its wheels.

'Let's wait and see what the crew thinks. We've only had the first aider's story so far.'

The small reprieve in decision-making gave Summer the chance to let her mind go further down that secret pathway.

She was more than a little bit in love with Zac Mitchell. Maybe it had started that night he'd winked at her across his grandmother's table last week. Or maybe it had started even before that—when he'd called that frightened elderly woman 'sweetheart' on that first job they'd ever done together.

The point of ignition didn't really matter now, anyway. What did matter was what happened next. She might want to take that next—huge—step of trusting him completely but it was debatable whether she was capable of it. Summer had no experience of going that far in a relationship but a lot of experience in pushing people away when she sensed any kind of a threat. She'd learned how to do that a very long time ago, when she'd only been a teenager. When she'd pushed her previously beloved father completely out of her life. She'd pushed other men away too, when they started to get too close.

That excuse of her career being more important wasn't really the truth at all, was it? She'd always had that whisper of warning that came in her mother's voice.

You can never trust a man. No matter how much you love them, it's never enough. They'll break your heart. Break you...

She was even pushing her best friend out of her life at the moment. There was a call she hadn't returned and a text message she'd brushed off with a breezy response that gave nothing away. Kate had no idea what was going on in Summer's life—that she was so far down the track of falling in love with the 'monster' who she believed had ruined her sister's life. Summer wasn't about to tell her, either. It was bad enough having the whisper of warning that was the haunting legacy her mother had left. Imagine adding the kind of poison that Kate couldn't help but administer, given her loyalty to Shelley? It would meld with that warning and she would have to start wondering if she was being as blind as her mother had been when she'd fallen in love so completely with her father.

That whole business with Shelley was a subject that she and Zac had put behind them by tacit consent and maybe she didn't want to hear what Kate had to say, anyway, because she wanted to trust Zac so much. She'd never met anyone remotely like him before and she instinctively knew that the odds of it happening again were non-existent.

This was her chance of finding out what it might be like. To be truly, utterly in love. And instinct was telling her more than how unique this situation was. Summer was also aware, on some level, that all it would require for her to take that final step of trust was to know that Zac felt the same way.

Telling Monty that she was prepared to put her life in Zac's hands on the end of the winch would have sent an unspoken response to that anticipation she'd sensed. It would have probably taken their newly forged bond to the next level—one that might have made it the right time to open their hearts a little further—but it wasn't going to happen today.

Another slow circuit in the blustery conditions and new information was available. The ground crew were going to scoop the patient and take him to the clearing. The patient was status two and was in respiratory distress but it wasn't a crush injury from the falling tree, as first reported.

It was far safer to land and preferable clinically, given that this was a chest injury and Zac could do more than any paramedic, but Summer was aware of a flash of disappointment. Had she wanted to publicly demonstrate the level of trust she had in Zac? Wanted the deeper kind of bond that would come from tackling—and winning— a tough challenge like this?

Never mind. It would no doubt come soon enough. And, in the meantime, they still had a challenge on their hands. A medical one.

'It's a penetrating wound,' the paramedic shouted over the noise of the slowing rotors as Zac and Summer ran, still crouching, towards the ambulance. 'The tree didn't land on him but it looks like he got stabbed with a branch or something. He's unresponsive. Now status one. Blood pressure's crashed and he's throwing off a lot of ectopics.'

This was an immediately life-threatening injury and it sounded as if a cardiac arrest was imminent. They worked fast and closely together as Summer intubated the young forestry worker and got IV fluids running as Zac performed the procedure she'd seen him do in Emergency on her car accident victim with the tension pneumothorax. But opening the chest cavity wasn't enough to allow the lungs to inflate, even when it had been done on both sides of the victim's chest.

'He's arrested.' Summer squeezed more oxygen in with the bag mask but this was looking hopeless. There was little point in starting external chest compressions when it was clear that there was some obstruction to the heart being able to fill and empty.

'The wound's within the nipple line on the left anterior chest.' Zac sounded calm but his tone was grim. 'It's not a pleural obstruction so it has to be pericardial. I'm going to open the chest with a clam shell thoracotomy.'

This was way beyond any procedure Summer could have performed. Beyond anything she'd seen in the emergency department, even. How confident would you have to be to actually open a chest in the field and expose a heart? But, if they didn't do something drastic, this young man was about to die.

Summer delegated the airway care to one of the ambulance paramedics so that she could work alongside Zac and pass him the necessary equipment. The sterilised strong scissors to extend the small opening that had been made in the hope of releasing trapped air or blood. The Gigli wire and forceps to cut through the breastbone. Rib spreaders to open the area and suction to clear it.

And then she watched, in amazement, as Zac used two clips to raise a tent of the covering around the heart and then cut a tiny hole before extending it. He used his gloved hands to remove massive blood clots. They could see the heart but it was still quivering ineffectually rather than beating.

Summer held her breath as Zac flicked the heart with his fingers. Once, then again, and she let her breath out in a sigh as she saw the heart contract. Fill and then contract again. She could feel the first effective beat as a pulse under her fingertips when she rested them on their patient's neck and a beep on the monitor behind them confirmed that a rhythm had recommenced. A movement of the whole chest was a first attempt by their patient to take a breath of his own.

Zac removed the rib spreaders and let the chest close.

'We'll put a sterile cover on this. We need to get him to Theatre stat.'

It still seemed like too big an ask to get their patient to hospital alive but, by some miracle, that was exactly what they managed to do. And, thanks to that achievement, the young forestry worker emerged from Theatre several hours later to go into intensive care. Still alive and looking as though he was going to stay that way.

It was all everyone could talk about, both in the emergency department of Auckland General and on the rescue helicopter base. It wasn't the first time such a major procedure had been attempted out of hospital but it was the first time it had had a successful outcome. Summer had never felt so proud of the job she did. Proud of the service she worked for. Proud of Zac...

'You're amazing, you know that?'

'So are you.'

They were still on base. Being professional colleagues. Nobody had guessed how close they'd become out of work hours yet and they were happy to keep it that way so all they could do right now was to hold eye contact long enough to communicate that the mutual appreciation went a lot deeper than anything professional. They would go over every tiny detail of this case, probably later this evening, and discuss the pros and cons of every choice and try to identify anything they could have done better. *Would* do better, if they were ever faced with a similar situation. She loved that they shared a passion for the same work. Being able to debrief a case in detail with Zac was taking Summer's clinical knowledge to a whole new level and she knew it was giving her an edge in her job that others were beginning to notice.

Maybe that wasn't the only thing that they were beginning to notice.

'What about me?' Monty sniffed. 'It wasn't exactly a ride in the park, flying in that weather, you know.'

'We couldn't have done it without you, mate.' Zac gave the pilot's shoulder a friendly thump as he went past. 'You're a legend.'

'We're all legends,' Summer said. 'How 'bout a beer after work to celebrate?'

'I've got a date already,' Monty said. 'You two go off on your own.' He returned Zac's friendly thump and grinned at Summer. 'You know you want to.'

'Um...' Summer could feel her cheeks redden. 'We just work well together.'

'Yeah...right. So how come you suck all the oxygen out of the air for the rest of us when you stand around making sheep's eyes at each other?'

'Did he really say that we were making sheep's eyes at each other?'

'Mmm.' Summer tilted her head to smile up at Zac. 'I believe he did.'

Zac grinned back and tightened his hold on Summer's hand as he helped her over the boulders on the beach and back onto the track they were following. For a while, they were silent, enjoying the shade of the heavy canopy of native bush and the sounds of the birdlife they had come here to see.

The journey itself had been a joy. Being on the road with Summer, seeing her bike in his rearview mirror, taking the corners like a faithful shadow. Riding a bike on the open road was always a pleasure but it could feel lonely. Being out with someone else changed the experience.

Being out with Summer Pearson changed everything. The sun seemed brighter. The smell of the sea as they stood outside on the ferry across to Tiritiri Matangi Island was fresher. Forgoing a guided tour so they could pretend they had the whole island to themselves had been a joint decision made with simply a heartbeat of eye contact. Walking hand in hand seemed like the most natural thing in the world. A pleasure shared being a pleasure doubled or something, maybe.

'What, exactly, *are* sheep's eyes?'

'Oh…you know…looking at each other for a bit too long, I guess. Like there's nobody else around.'

'I've always thought sheep were not particularly intelligent creatures.'

Summer laughed—a delicious ripple of sound that Zac immediately wanted to hear again.

'Are we being stupid, do you think?'

The glance he received was startled. 'How do you mean?'

'It's not against the rules, is it? To get involved with a fellow crew member? A colleague?'

Summer shook her head and her chuckle was

rueful. 'If it was, you'd all be in trouble in the emergency department, wouldn't you?'

'It's a bit different on the choppers, though. Much tighter teams.'

'We're all adults. We get to make our own choices and deal with any consequences. The only trouble would be if you let something personal interfere with anything professional.' Summer dropped his hand as she climbed up a set of narrow steps that was part of a boardwalk. 'I'm surprised that anyone guessed about us so fast, though. I thought we were being really discreet.'

'Apparently we suck all the oxygen out of the room.' Zac's tone was light but he knew exactly what Monty had been referring to. Sometimes, it felt that way when he was looking at Summer. As if he'd forgotten how to breathe or something. A weird sensation that he'd never experienced before.

Good weird, though—he was pretty sure about that.

'Do you think Ivy knows?'

'Well...you know how you and Flint stayed

around the other night, after we'd been out for that swim?'

'Mmm?' Something in her tone suggested that Summer was remembering how amazing the second time together had been. Any first time awkwardness had vanished and they had been ready to play. To get to know each other's bodies and revel in the pleasure they knew they could both give and receive.

'When I popped in to say good morning before I went to work the next day, she gave me a pile of new towels. Said that mine were old enough to feel like cardboard and they simply weren't suitable for delicate skin. I don't think she was referring to *my* skin.'

'But I snuck out well before dawn. It was still dark by the time Flint and I had jogged back to the boat.'

Zac threw a wry smile over his shoulder. 'There's not much that gets past Gravy. She's had ninety plus years to hone her skills, after all.'

'Oh... Do you think she disapproves?'

'If she did, I don't think she'd be supplying soft

towels. She'd think that the cardboard variety would be a suitable penance. Oh...look at that.'

They had come to one of the feeding stations on the island. Cleverly designed platforms supported bottles of sugar water. This station had attracted both bellbirds and tuis and, for several minutes, they both stood entranced, watching. The bellbirds were small and elegant, the tuis much larger and more confident—the white ruff on their necks being shown off as they reached to sip the water from the metal tubes.

They saw stitchbirds and riflemen further along the track and then the highlight they would be talking about for days came when a group of takahe crossed their path. The huge flightless birds with their blue and green plumage and big red beaks were fascinating.

'They thought they were extinct, you know. Like the moas. There's only a few places you can see them now. This is a first for me.'

'Me, too.' Summer's face was alight with pleasure. 'This was such a good idea, Zac. And I thought we were just going for a bike ride.'

'I'm full of good ideas.' Zac caught her hand as they started walking again. 'Stick around long enough and you'll find out.'

'I might just do that.'

Her words stayed in the air as they walked on. Zac could still hear them when they finally sat on the grass near the lighthouse to eat the picnic they'd put together from the shop near the ferry terminal. They were hungry enough after all the walking to polish off the filled rolls and muffins and fruit and then they lay back in the long grass. They had some time to spare before walking back down the hill to catch the ferry back.

It was inevitable that they started kissing. They were lying so close together, well away from any other visitors to the island. It was a gorgeous day and they had been having the best time in each other's company. The kisses were sweet. Perfect. Was that why Zac was aware of a warning bell sounding?

'It feels like we're breaking the rules,' he finally confessed.

'But we only work together sometimes. It's not like we're even employed by the same people.'

'I didn't mean that.' Zac propped himself up on one elbow but Summer had closed her eyes against the glare of the sun, a hand shading her face. 'I mean my own rules.'

Summer spread her fingers and peered up at him. 'You have rules?'

'Kind of.'

'What kind of rules?'

'Like not getting in too deep.'

'Oh...' She was really looking at him now but he couldn't read her expression. If he had to guess, he might say she looked wary. Almost afraid?

He had to kiss her again. To reassure her. Or maybe he was trying to reassure himself?

'This feels different. Weird.'

Her lips quirked with a tiny smile. 'Good weird or bad weird?'

'I think...good weird.'

'But you don't know?'

Zac sucked in a breath. Had he ever been this

honest with a woman before? 'I do know. I'm just not sure I trust it. Because it's...too good?'

A single nod from Summer. She understood.

'I've never had a good role model for what can be trusted,' Zac said quietly. 'My grandad died before I could remember him and my stepfather... well, I prefer not to remember him.'

Summer nodded again. 'My parents weren't exactly a shining example to follow either.' She sat up, as if even thinking about her family had disturbed her. Zac wanted to ask about what had gone so wrong but he didn't want to spoil this moment because it felt important. A step forward.

'But we're adults,' he said. 'We get to make our own choices, don't we? And live with the consequences.'

'How do you know if you're making the right choices, though?'

'I guess you don't. I think that maybe you have to do what feels right and then hope that you *have* made the right ones.'

Did she understand what he was trying to say

here, or was he being too clumsy? He didn't want to scare her off completely.

He didn't seem to have done that. If it had been a declaration of sorts, then Summer seemed to be in complete agreement. She stretched out her arms and linked them around his neck, pulling him towards her for another kiss.

'This feels right,' she murmured. 'Weird but good.'

Better than good. It felt as if they had agreed to make this choice. That there was a potential to trust on both sides. Almost an unspoken promise that they would both do their best for whatever was happening between them not to become an emotional disaster.

Inevitably, the real world had to intrude again. Zac checked his watch as he became aware that they really were alone here now. 'We've got two minutes and then we need to head back fast for the ferry. Gravy would be upset if we don't get back for the dinner she's cooking up for us.'

Her lips were moving against his. 'We'd better make the most of them then, hadn't we?'

* * *

'There you go, Gravy. A nice hot lemon drink to wash down that paracetamol. You'll feel better in no time.'

'I just hope I didn't give Summer this cold when she was here for dinner the other night after you'd been out to the bird island.'

'I think she's pretty tough. She'll survive.'

Ivy sniffed her drink. 'You know, I think a hot toddy might work faster. With a good slosh of whisky.'

'Hmm.' Zac took a mohair rug off the back of the couch and held it up but Ivy shook her head.

'Far too hot for that. Summer colds are the worst.' Ivy blew her nose and leaned back in her chair but she was smiling. 'Summer,' she murmured. 'Such a lovely name. Conjures up the feeling of blue skies and sunshine, doesn't it? The sparkle of the sea and long, delicious evenings to enjoy it.'

'Is there anything else I can do for you before I head downstairs?'

'Sit and talk to me for a minute. Unless you're meeting your Summer?'

'Not tonight.' Zac settled himself on the couch beside his grandmother. 'She's doing some crew training. And we don't spend every minute of our time off together, anyway.'

'You'll have to bring her to dinner with me again soon. I ordered some new champagne on-line yesterday and it looks lovely. I could do your favourite roast chicken.'

'You're not to do anything for a few days except rest and get better. If that cough gets any worse, I'll be having a chat to your GP. You might need some antibiotics.'

'I'll be fine. I can't have been eating enough garlic, that's what it is.'

'Maybe you should stop swimming when the weather isn't so good. I saw you out in the rain the other day.'

Ivy snorted. 'You know as well as I do that the weather doesn't cause a viral infection.'

'Getting cold lowers your resistance.'

Ivy flapped a hand in his direction. 'I'll stop swimming when I'm dead, thanks very much, and who knows how far away that is? I intend to make the most of every day I've got.'

'Don't say that.' Zac frowned. 'I expect you to be around for a long time yet.'

Ivy's smile was unusually gentle. 'Nobody lives for ever, darling.'

Zac smiled back and took hold of one of her hands. When had her skin started to feel so papery and fragile? An internal alarm was sounding faintly. This was what it was like when you had somebody who was this important to you. You had to live with the fear of losing them. His gran was all the more precious because of that knowledge he'd come by too early in life.

'You could try.' There was a tight feeling in his throat. 'You're my touchstone, Gravy. I don't even want to think about what life will be like when you're not around.'

'Maybe you've found a new touchstone.' Ivy turned her hand over and gave his a squeeze. 'Your little ray of summer sunshine.'

'You wouldn't have thought that the first time

I met her. She's not only tough. She can be quite fierce.'

'Good.' Ivy sipped her hot drink. 'Being fierce is an attribute. Sometimes you have to fight in life to get through things. And it sounds like she's had to get through more than her fair share. Not that she said much, but it sounded like her mum was the only family she had and she lost her when she was far too young.'

'Mmm...' He'd had the opportunity to ask more about her background when they'd been on the island but he'd held back. Boundaries were still being respected. On both sides? Was that a good thing—or another warning?

'She's got a heart of gold, that girl,' Ivy said quietly. 'And she loves you to bits.'

'You think...?'

'It's obvious from where I'm standing. And I think you feel the same way.'

Zac pushed his fingers through his hair. That would certainly explain why this felt so different. 'Maybe...'

'But?'

'Who said there was a but?'

'You only mess up your hair like that when you can't decide something. You've been doing it since you were a little boy, Isaac. I always had to carry a comb whenever we went out anywhere.'

'Hmm. It's early days, I guess.'

Ivy snorted. 'Nonsense. When something's right, it's right. You should know by now.'

'I don't want to rush into anything.'

'You're already into it up to your eyebrows, from what I can see.'

Zac couldn't deny it. He'd never felt this way about any girl before but… Yes, there was a but…

'Maybe it's her independence that bothers me,' he admitted. 'How different she is. How many girls live by themselves on a boat? Ride a motorbike and kick ass in a job that would be too much for most people to cope with?'

'*Language*, Isaac. Please.'

'Sorry. But she's amazing at what she does. She's got this confidence that makes you think she'd cope with anything by herself. And yes, she probably did have to cope with too much when she was young. But would she want to fight to keep a relationship together if times got tough or would she just walk away and cope all by herself again?'

Ivy sniffed. 'Sounds like the pot calling the kettle black, Isaac Mitchell. How many relationships have you walked out on so far when they didn't go the way you wanted them to? When they wanted more than you were ready to give? You've broken your share of hearts, you know.'

'It wasn't intentional.'

'I know that.' Ivy patted his hand. 'And you were always very kind about it.'

'I've just never found the person that makes me want to give everything I could to.' But he had now, hadn't he? The only thing stopping him was a fear of...what? Having his heart broken? Again?

Ivy was giving him a look that said she understood. That she remembered the small boy whose world had crumbled when he'd lost his mother. But it was also a look that told him it was time to be brave enough to break his own rules. The ones about working hard and playing hard and guarding your heart. That she knew exactly who the person was. A look that suggested he was being just a little bit obtuse.

Zac felt the need to defend himself. 'You only got married once,' he reminded her. 'I'm cut from the same cloth. If I give everything, it'll only happen once. I think if the trust it takes to do that gets broken, you never find it again. Never as much. So it has to be right.'

Ivy's gaze was misty. Was she remembering the love of her life, who'd sadly been taken before Zac was old enough to remember him?

'Nothing's ever perfect, darling. At some point you have to take a leap of faith and hope for the best. I hope you'll be as lucky as I was. But don't wait too long.' She closed her eyes as she leaned her head back against a cushion. 'I want to see you waiting for your bride at the end of the aisle. I want to throw confetti and drink a wee bit too much champagne and be disgracefully tipsy by the end of the reception.' She opened her eyes again and the expression in them gave Zac that tight feeling in his throat again. This time it felt like a rock with sharp edges.

'I want to know that you'll be living here in this house and there'll be babies playing in the garden and building sandcastles on the beach. Dogs tracking sand into the house and maybe a paddleboard or two propped up against that dusty old boatshed.'

Zac found his own eyes closing for a long blink. He could almost see it himself.

And it looked...perfect.

CHAPTER SEVEN

THE MORE TIME he spent with Summer, the more Zac could see that picture of a perfect future.

'D'you think you'll always want to live on a boat?' The query was casual. They were restocking gear during a quiet spell one afternoon.

'No way. I had no idea I'd be doing it for *this* long.' Summer turned to look at the pouch Zac was filling. 'Have you got plenty of size eight cuffed tracheal tubes in there?'

'Three. That's enough, isn't it?'

'Yes. Make sure we've got sizes three, four and five of the laryngeal mask airways, too. And we'll do the paediatric airway kit next.'

'Sure.' Zac checked the size printed on the sterile packages for the LMAs. 'So how long did you think you'd live on a boat, then?'

'As long as it took to save up a house deposit.'

She snapped a laryngoscope handle into place to check the light and then folded it closed again. 'I was looking for a share flat when I moved up from Hamilton but then I heard about the boat and it was cheaper. I didn't expect house prices to go so crazy, though. It feels like I'm getting further and further away. And living on the boat's not helping.'

'Even if it's cheaper?'

'I'm getting spoiled. I can't imagine living far from a beach now and they're always the pricier suburbs.'

'I know. My grandparents had no idea what a good investment they were making when they bought a rundown old house on the beach nearly sixty years ago.'

'It's a perfect house.'

Zac opened the paediatric airway kit. He ran his gaze over the shiny laryngoscope blades and handles, the Magill forceps and the range of tracheal tubes and LMAs. There didn't seem to be anything missing from the slots. He checked the pocket that held the tiniest airways that could be needed in resuscitating a newborn baby and sent out a silent prayer that they wouldn't be needing to use any of them any time soon.

A quick glance at Summer took in the way she was sitting cross-legged on the storeroom floor. She had another kit open on her lap—the serious airway gear that made things like scalpels and tracheal dilators available when all else failed.

Her words still echoed in the back of his head.

The house that he would inherit one day was *perfect*. Like the life that Ivy had imagined him living in it one day.

He'd always loved the house but how much better was it on the nights that Summer and Flint stayed over? When they could all go out at first light and run on the beach or brave the cold water for an early morning wake-up swim?

It was like his job. Perfect but so much better when he got to share it with Summer. The bonus of seeing the crew in their orange flight suits arrive to hand over a patient when he was on a shift in Emergency always added something special to his day. Days like today, when he was actually working on the rescue base as her crew partner, were the best of all.

Ivy's warning of not waiting too long had been surfacing more and more in recent days.

He was coasting. Enjoying each day as it came. Trusting that it would continue for as long as they both wanted it to. Trusting that it was safe to give more and more because it could become stronger and potentially last for the rest of his life.

And there was the rub. He might be confident that Summer felt the same way he did but he couldn't be sure until he heard her say it out loud. And maybe she was waiting for him to say something first? Something else Ivy had said had struck home. He was the pot calling the kettle black. Maybe he and Summer were more alike than he'd realised. They both had the kind of skills that came from putting so much effort into their work. They chose leisure activities like ocean sports and riding powerful bikes that meant they could play as hard as they worked. Perhaps Summer's fierce independence came from self-protection and it would take something extraordinary to persuade her to remove the barriers that were protecting her heart?

But what they had found together was extraordinary, wasn't it? Surely he couldn't be the only one feeling like this?

The buzzing of their pagers broke the silence. Kits were rolled up and stuffed back into the pack with swift movements. They were both on their feet within seconds. Strapped into their seats in the helicopter within minutes. Heading west.

'Piha Beach,' Monty confirmed. 'ETA ten minutes.'

'I've been there for near-drownings,' Summer said. 'And falls from the rocks. I can't believe someone's been attacked by a shark.'

'We're being followed,' Monty told them. 'Reckon you'll both be starring on the national news tonight.'

Zac knew he would recognise the landmarks below with ease. Lion Rock was famous. Lying forty kilometres west of the city, Piha was the most famous surf beach in the country.

'I used to surf at Piha when I was a kid,' he

told Summer. 'When I got my first wheels when I was seventeen, I chose an old Combi van and me and my mates were in heaven. We'd load up the boards and wetsuits before dawn and we'd get home, sunburned and completely exhausted, well after dark. There was always a big roast dinner on offer when we got back. It was no wonder I was so popular at school.'

The look he was getting from Summer suggested that there were other reasons he might have been popular. Her gaze held his with a tenderness that made something ache deep in his chest and her smile made it feel like whatever it was had just split open to release some kind of hitherto untried drug.

Love. That was what it was, all right.

Summer *did* feel the same way he did—he was sure of it. And he'd never loved anyone this much. Never would ever again. It was time he did something about making sure he never lost it. For both their sakes, he needed to be brave and be the first one to take those barriers away. To put his heart on the line.

The first chance he got—tonight—he was going to tell Summer how he felt. Maybe even ask her to move in with him.

Marry him...?

Whoa...where had *that* notion come from? And now that it was here, it was the weirdest thought ever—maybe because it felt so right. The knowledge was fleeting, however. It couldn't claim even another second of headspace as the distinctive shape of Lion Rock—the formation that separated the two beaches at Piha—loomed larger.

Zac could see the knot of people on the beach below, including the red and yellow uniforms of the lifeguards, and many more were watching from a distance. Several bystanders were waving their arms, urging the rescue crew to land as quickly as possible. There was nobody in the water, surfing or swimming. It could be a while before this popular beach could be deemed safe, despite a shark attack in New Zealand being an extraordinarily rare occurrence.

One of the lifeguards met them as they raced

from the helicopter over the firm sand they'd been able to land on.

'We've got the bleeding under control with a pressure bandage but he's lost a lot of blood. And his leg's a real mess, man... I hope he's not going to lose it.'

'Is he conscious?' The priority was keeping this patient alive, not discussing a potential prognosis. It sounded like preservation of blood volume was likely to be the key management, along with as swift a transfer to hospital as possible.

'He swam in himself with his board, yelling for help, but he was barely conscious by the time we got him onto the beach. We've got oxygen on and put some blankets over him to try and keep him warm and he's woken up a bit. He's in a lot of pain.'

The knot of people—including a skinny lad gripping a surfboard that had obvious tooth marks and a chunk bitten out of its end—parted to let Zac and Summer into the centre and place their packs on the sand. Summer immediately dropped to her knees to open the pack and start extracting gear they would need, like a blood pressure cuff and IV supplies. She reached for the man's wrist as Zac crouched by the patient's head.

'No radial pulse palpable,' she said.

The man looked to be in his early fifties and he was deathly pale but breathing well and Zac could feel a rapid pulse beneath his fingers from the carotid artery in his neck. It was a lot fainter than he would have liked and if it wasn't reaching his wrist it meant that his blood pressure was already dangerously low. Hypovolaemic shock was a life-threatening emergency and they might have to fight to keep this man alive. From the corner of his eye, Zac could see Summer unrolling the IV kit. She would be putting a tourniquet on and aiming to get a cannula in and IV fluids running as quickly as she could.

'Hey, buddy.' Zac shook the man's shoulder. 'Can you open your eyes for me?' Response to voice was a good indication of level of consciousness and he was relieved to see the man's eyelids flutter open and get a groan of verbal response.

Zac glanced up at the onlookers. 'Does anyone know his name?'

An affirmative chorus sounded from all sides.

'It's Jon,' one of the lifeguards told him. 'He's one of us—a Patrol Captain.'

'Jon Pearson,' someone else called. 'He's fifty-two. Lives locally.'

Pearson?

Startled, Zac's gaze swerved towards Summer and—just for a heartbeat—his focus was broken by regretting not taking that opportunity he'd had to find out more about her background. He really needed to know more than he did right now.

What little information he had flashed through his brain with astonishing speed. Her parents had been hippies. She'd been conceived on a beach in the wake of a surfing competition. She had no siblings. Her mother had died when she was seventeen and her father was already 'well out of the picture'. Her parents had not been 'a shining example' of something to follow as far as relationships went. What had she meant by that?

*Dear God…*had there been violence involved? Had she had to cope with the same sort of fear in her childhood as he had?

More importantly in this moment, however, if this man *was* Summer's father—and that seemed quite likely given that he was a surfer—how was she coping, seeing him for the first time in so many years, let alone in a life-threatening emergency? Having to treat him? It was a paramedic's worst nightmare, having to treat a loved one. How much harder could it be if the relationship was complicated and emotionally distressing anyway?

She seemed to be coping. She had a tourniquet around their patient's arm and was swabbing the skin on his arm.

'You'll feel a sharp scratch,' she warned. 'There. All done.' The cannula slid home into the vein and Summer released the tourniquet and reached for the connection so that she could hook up the bag of IV fluid she had ready.

And then she looked up and caught Zac's steady gaze as he did his best to communicate silently.

I understand, he tried to tell her. *I'm here for you. I'll do whatever it takes to help.*

She could do this. She could cope.

She *had* to.

It had almost done her in, though, that first instant she'd seen their patient's face. Of course she had recognised him—despite the differences that fifteen years had etched onto his face. For one horrible moment, she had frozen—assaulted by a flashback of the grief she'd had to deal with all those years ago when he'd chosen to walk out of her life.

The only way to deal with it had been to blank out those memories. The visceral knowledge that this was her only living relative. He had to become simply another patient. A man with hypovolaemic shock who was in urgent need of fluid replacement. All she had to think about was putting a large bore cannula into his arm and to get fluids running. Probably two IV lines—except that it was equally important to find out whether the loss of blood was actually as controlled as the first aiders had led them to believe.

'I don't like the staining on that pressure bandage,' she told Zac. 'It could be soaking up volume.'

Zac nodded. 'Have a look at what's going on.' He was still crouching beside her father's head. 'Jon? You still with us, mate? Open your eyes…'

'*Hurts*,' Jon groaned. 'My *leg*…'

'I'm going to give you something for the pain.'

Summer used shears to cut away the bandage. The ripped flesh on Jon's thigh was horrific. She could see the gleam of exposed bone in one patch and…yes…there was a small spurt of an arterial bleed still going on. She clamped her gloved fingers over the vessel and pressed hard.

Jon groaned and then swore vehemently. Summer had to close her eyes for a heartbeat as the cry of pain ripped its way through the emotional wall she had erected.

This was just another patient. *Jon*. Not Dad. Sometimes you had to cause pain to save a life. It didn't make it harder because he was her father. He wasn't her father any more. He hadn't been for fifteen years…

She opened her eyes as she sucked in a new breath, to find Zac looking up from where he was filling a syringe from an ampoule. He was giving her that look again. The one that told her he had somehow made the connection the moment he'd heard their patient's name and that he knew exactly how hard this was. How much he wanted to make it easier for her.

He knew nothing about her history and yet he was prepared to take her side and protect her from someone who had the potential to be some kind of threat. Funny how she could still be so focused on what she had to do but be aware of how much she loved this man. How easy it would be to put her emotional safety in his hands for ever.

'The femoral artery's been nicked,' she said. 'I'm putting some pressure on it.'

'We might need to clamp it. I'll get some pain relief on board first.'

Yes. Knock him out, Summer thought. The pain of what she was doing had roused him. Any second now and he was going to look to see what was happening and…

'*Summer?*' The word was shocked. Disbelieving. Jon pulled at the oxygen mask on his face as if he wanted to make his speech more audible. 'Is that…*you?*'

'Keep your mask on, mate.' A lifeguard crouching at his head pushed the mask back into place.

The guard holding the bag of IV fluid aloft crouched to catch his arm. 'Keep your arm still, Jon. You don't want the line to come out.'

During the flurry of activity, Zac injected the pain relief and Jon relaxed, his arms dropping and his eyes closing. A flash of eye contact told her that Zac was relieved that things hadn't got any more difficult but it did nothing to interrupt his focus on what they had to do as soon as possible—to get this bleeding under control so that pouring fluids in to maintain blood pressure wasn't a futile exercise.

Forceps were a good enough temporary measure to close the artery. Sterile dressings covered the wound. It took only a few minutes to have their patient packaged onto the stretcher and stable enough to fly.

'Any family or close friends here?' Zac asked.

Summer deliberately avoided making eye contact with anybody. How many people had heard him say her name? The name that was embroidered on her overalls for anybody to check. A name that was unusual enough to be an accusation if someone knew that Jon had had a daughter in a previous life. It was normal to find out whether there was anyone who might want to travel with a patient who was seriously injured, anyway. These could be the last moments they had together.

'Me.' The skinny kid who'd been standing there, silently gripping the damaged surfboard, spoke up. 'I'm Dylan. He's my dad.'

She didn't manage to avoid Zac's glance this time. He was hiding it well but he was shocked. Did he think she'd known she had a half-brother? *Oh, man*...he couldn't be as shocked as she was. A half-*brother*?

She tried to shove the thought aside. This was

her father's new family. It didn't have to have anything to do with her, other than as a professional. They couldn't just take a boy who didn't look any older than about ten or eleven with them. He would need to travel with an adult.

'Where's your mum?' The words came out more fiercely than she would have chosen.

'Haven't got one.'

'She died,' someone said quietly, close to Summer's shoulder. 'Couple of years back.'

'There's just me and my dad.'

The boy had blue eyes. And they were dark with distress—making him look a lot older than he probably was. A lot older than any kid should have to look. Summer had lost her mother. She knew what that was like but she couldn't afford to start feeling sorry for the kid. If she let him touch her heart, it might open the door to everything associated with her father and that was a world of hurt she thought she'd left well in the past.

But how could she not feel the connection? This kid even *looked* like her. Short and skinny, with bleached blond hair that was probably still full of sea water, which was why it was sticking up all over the place in the kind of spikes that Summer favoured for a hairstyle.

The unexpected mix of something so personal with what should have been a purely professional situation was impossible to deal with. Thank goodness Zac seemed to know exactly the right way to deal with it. He had his hand on a skinny shoulder.

'Want to come with us, then? We'll look after you, buddy.'

A single nod. The surfboard was handed over, with some reverence, to one of the lifeguards. The news crew, who'd been filming from a respectable distance, began to move closer. People would get interviewed. Close-up shots of that surfboard would probably be all over the Internet in no time. There could be more reporters waiting at the hospital and they'd be eager to get some sound bites from one of the crew.

Maybe Monty could deal with that. Or Graham, back at the base. All Summer wanted to do was get this job over with and find some way of getting her head around it all. But what was she going to do about the boy? She had a responsibility, whether she wanted it or not, and dealing with that was inevitably going to open a can of worms that Zac would want to talk about. That he had the right to know about, even?

A short time later, Dylan was strapped into the front seat of the helicopter beside Monty, and Zac and Summer were in the back with their patient. They were lifting off from the beach. They were in an environment totally familiar to Summer and heading back to the world she knew and loved.

But it didn't feel the same any more.

It was being shaken and it was impossible to know just how much damage might be happening.

Even Zac seemed different. Was it her imagination or was he treating Jon with even more care than usual? She didn't need reminding to keep a constant watch on his blood pressure and oxygen saturation. Surely he didn't need to keep asking about pain levels?

'It's down to three out of ten,' she finally snapped. 'And we're only a few minutes away from hospital. He doesn't need any more pain relief.'

Zac's expression was sympathetic but it felt like a reprimand. He was trying to do the best for everyone involved here but this was a decision their patient should be allowed to make. Was he providing an example of not letting anything personal interfere with something professional? 'How bad is it, Jon?'

'Better than before.' It was clearly an effort for him to open his eyes. 'Summer?'

It was easy to pretend to be absorbed in the measurements she was recording. To pretend she hadn't heard him call her name.

'Where's my boy?' Jon asked then. 'Who's looking after Dylan?'

'He's up front,' Zac told him. 'Coming to the hospital with us.'

'But who's going to look after him? He's just a kid...'

'Don't worry about it,' Zac said. 'I'll make sure he's taken good care of.'

What? Summer's frown was fierce. This felt wrong. This wasn't what he'd promised in that look. The one that had told her he was on her side and would protect her. He was treating Jon Pearson as if he was his girlfriend's father and not just a potential threat to her emotional wellbeing. As if this unknown and unwelcome halfsibling was part of her family.

And what did that say about Zac? That he'd think it was forgivable to cheat on your wife for pretty much an entire marriage? That it was okay to pack a bag and simply walk out when you decided that your daughter was old enough to be considered an adult?

'You're grown up now, chicken. It shouldn't matter that me and your mum aren't going to live together any longer. I won't be far away. I'll always be your dad.'

She'd only just turned sixteen, for heaven's sake. She'd been nowhere near old enough to handle her mother's emotional disintegration.

And it sure as hell *had* mattered.

'You're a cheat. A lying cheat. I can't believe you'd do this to Mum. To me. I hate you...I never want to see you again...'

She had seen him again, though, hadn't she? At her mother's funeral, less than a year later. Not that she'd gone anywhere near him. What could she have said?

This was your fault. It might not look like it to anyone else but, as far as I'm concerned, it was murder...

Murder by drowning in the dank blackness of the cloud that had been left behind in their lives.

The echo of her mother's voice was even more disturbing. Concentrating on recording a new set of figures wasn't enough to chase it away.

Blood pressure was ninety over sixty. Improving. At least it was recordable now.

You can never trust a man... No matter how much you love them—it's never enough...

Oxygen saturation was ninety-three per cent. Not enough but it had also improved from what it had been. There was enough blood—albeit pretty diluted now—to be keeping Jon alive.

'He's going to need blood.' Had Zac guessed her train of thought? 'Do you happen to know his group? Might speed things up.'

'He's O positive.'

'Really? Me, too.'

The coincidence was hardly impressive. 'So am I. It is the most common group, you know. Thirty-eight per cent of people are O positive.'

Her tone sounded off, even to her own ears. Cold, even. She turned to stare at the cardiac monitor.

He was in sinus rhythm so his heart was coping. The heart rate was too fast at a hundred and twenty but that was only to be expected with the low levels of circulating oxygen.

Looking up at the monitor made it inevitable that her glance would slide sideways at Zac but he'd looked away when she'd been making the comment about blood groups and seemed to be focused on checking the dressings over Jon's leg wound.

She couldn't shake that echo of her mother's voice. How could she when her father was lying there only inches away from her?

She loved Zac. More than she would have ever believed it was possible to love someone. And she trusted him completely.

Despite evidence to the contrary? How easily had she taken his word and shut those poisonous whispers from Kate out of her life?

The way her mother had always refused to believe rumours of her father's infidelity?

Her thoughts shouldn't be straying like this in the middle of a job. She was being unprofessional. She'd never felt like this. Well—maybe just a little—that first day she'd been on the job with Zac and she'd had to make an effort to separate the personal and professional, but that paled in comparison to the wash of mixed emotions she couldn't control right now. A mix of the present and past that was turning into a confused jumble.

Shaking things unbearably. Damaging things.

Nothing was going to be quite the same after this. Including how she felt about Zac?

Maybe that was the worst thing about it.

They were coming in to land on the roof of Auckland General. There would be a resus team waiting for them in Emergency. They could hand their patient over and if it had been any normal job that would be the end of it.

But Summer knew that, this time, it might only be the beginning of something else.

Something that had the potential to ruin her life all over again?

How on earth was she going to cope?

And then they were out of the helicopter and there was a flurry of activity as they got everybody out and ready to move. Summer gathered up the paperwork so she was a step behind as the stretcher started to roll. A nurse had taken charge of Dylan. For a moment, Summer stared at the entourage and it was hard to make her feet move to start following them.

But somehow Zac was right beside her. His side pressed against hers.

'It's okay,' he told her. 'We can deal with this. All of it.'

It was a good thing they had to move fast to catch up with their patient and take the lift down to the emergency department. A good thing that there were so many other people around because otherwise Summer might have burst into tears.

She had no idea exactly how they were going to deal with any of this but she desperately wanted to believe Zac.

There was the most enormous relief in the idea that, this time, she wasn't going to have to do this alone.

They could deal with this.

Together.

CHAPTER EIGHT

ZAC STOOD WITH Dylan in the corner of the resuscitation room, his arm around the boy's shoulders, as the team made their initial assessment of his father. Summer stood on the boy's other side. Not touching him but still close.

He could only imagine the mixed feelings she must be experiencing but she was standing her ground. Being protective of a scared ten-year-old kid who she happened to be related to. It made Zac feel enormously proud of her.

'Do a type and cross match,' Rob told one of the nurses. 'He's going to need a transfusion.'

'He's O positive,' Zac said.

'Thanks, mate, but we'll still have to check.' Rob's glance took in how close Zac and Summer were standing to Dylan but, if he was surprised, he gave no sign of it, with the same kind of professionalism that had stopped any of the team commenting that their patient's name was the same as Summer's. 'Bitten by a shark, huh? Your dad's going to have a great story to tell, isn't he?'

'Is he…is he going to be okay?'

'We're going to give him some more blood and make sure he's stable and then he'll be going up to the operating theatre so they can see what they can do. Try not to worry too much, okay?' Rob's smile was reassuring but he turned away swiftly. 'Has someone got hold of Orthopaedics yet? And where's the neurosurgical registrar? And Summer…?'

'Yes?' Summer responded to the tilt of the ED consultant's head. He wanted a private word. Was he going to warn her that Dylan might need to be prepared for the worst? That he might lose his father?

That she might lose her father again—permanently, this time?

It shouldn't make any difference but it did. There was new grief to be found. A grief mixed with regret and…and something that felt like… *shame*?

'We need to intubate,' Rob told her quietly. 'It's better if you take the lad somewhere else. Is he… is there some connection I should know about?'

Summer's heart was thumping. This was the moment when she had to decide how far she was going to go in opening a part of her life that had previously been out of bounds.

'Jon Pearson is my father,' she said aloud. 'And Dylan's my half-brother. I… I didn't know he existed before today, though.'

'Hmm…' Rob's look was searching. 'You okay?'

Summer's gaze shifted to where Zac was still standing with his arm around Dylan's shoulders. Skinny shoulders that were hunched in misery and fear.

'I think I will be,' she said quietly.

'I'll get Mandy to set up one of the relatives' rooms for you. She can take care of him if you need a break for any reason. If there's any way we can help, just say.'

Dylan wasn't happy about being taken somewhere else.

'I want to stay with my dad.' There was hostility in the glare being delivered as she and Zac ushered him out of the resus room. 'I don't want to go anywhere with you. You're Summer. I know all about you. You were mean to Dad.'

Summer's jaw dropped. *She* had been mean?

'Um...I didn't know about you.'

'You would have if you'd talked to Dad. Like he'd always wanted you to.'

Summer tried to push away memories of things she wasn't proud of. Like the look on her father's face when she'd turned her back on him at the funeral and walked away. The letters she had ripped up. The parcels she'd had returned to their sender. Yes...there was definitely shame to be found in the kaleidoscope of emotions this day was creating.

'You don't care,' Dylan continued. 'You don't care if Dad dies. You don't care about *me*.'

'That's not true.' The sincerity in her words was a shock because it *was* genuinely sincere. She'd had no idea how much she *did* actually care, did she? But there was a huge part of her that still didn't *want* to care. There was a battle going on inside and it was hard to know which way to turn.

'He's not going to die, buddy.' Zac's voice was calm. 'What we don't know is whether they're going to be able to save his leg and we're not going to know that for a while yet. You can't stay while the doctors are doing their work and that's why we're taking you somewhere else. In here. Look, there's a TV and DVDs and that machine has lots of food.'

'Are you going to stay with me?'

'Sure.' Zac's smile was as reassuring as his calmness.

'So *she* doesn't need to stay then, does she?'

'She kind of does.' Zac let the door swing closed behind them.

'Why?'

'Well…she's kind of your big sister.'

Dylan's huff was dismissive and Summer could feel herself stiffen defensively. So what if this kid didn't want anything to do with her? Maybe she didn't want anything to do with him, either. She was just trying to do the right thing, here.

'And we're kind of together, you know?'

'You mean she's your girlfriend?'

'Yeah...' Zac's gaze found Summer's and held it. She felt some of the tension ebb away. Yes, there was a battle going on but she wasn't alone and if she had the choice of anyone to be on her side, she would choose this man.

Dylan's gaze went from Zac to Summer and back again. He shrugged and the look he gave Zac was an attempt at a man-to-man resignation that could have been funny if it wasn't heart-breaking at the same time.

'Guess that's okay, then.'

An hour of waiting brought the news that Jon had been taken into Theatre. Another hour passed and then another. The team of specialists had a huge job ahead of them to try and repair nerves and blood vessels and muscle if they were going to save his leg. Dylan had stopped talking as soon as the decision had been made regarding his company and all Zac and Summer could do was sit there with him and watch the cartoons he'd chosen as distraction.

Shared glances acknowledged how much they needed to talk about but none of it could be discussed in front of Dylan. Even the practicalities of where he would stay while his father was in hospital was something that needed to wait until they had confirmation that all had gone well in Theatre. The young boy seemed oblivious to the tension and frustration that slowly built around him. He shut himself away, seemingly absorbed by the meaningless entertainment, until, eventually, he fell deeply asleep on the couch. Mandy chose a moment a short time later to poke her head around the door.

'Looks like he's out for the count.'

'Yeah. Any word from upstairs?'

'Sounds like it got a bit dodgy for a while. He lost a huge amount of blood. Last I heard, he's stable again and the neurosurgeons are doing their bit.' Mandy took a blanket from the back of the couch and covered Dylan's bare legs. 'Why don't you two take a break? I'll stay in here with him. Even after his dad gets to Recovery it's going to be another hour or two before he'll be awake enough for a visitor.'

Zac stood up. 'Great idea. Let's go and get some coffee, Summer.' She looked exhausted enough to fall asleep herself but the lines of tension in her face suggested that was unlikely to be an option for a long while. She needed to talk more than she needed to sleep, but how much would she be prepared to tell him?

The sensation of being nervous was unexpected but this was a big ask, wasn't it? How close would Summer let him get?

How much did she really trust him?

He couldn't just ask, either. He knew that Summer guarded her privacy. He knew that he would probably get some answers by asking direct questions but he didn't want to do that. The information would still be guarded and the question of trust would not be answered. It mattered whether Summer was prepared to tell him what was important without being asked. Trust was like love, wasn't it? If it wasn't given freely—if you had to *ask* for it—it probably wasn't really worth having.

And it didn't seem as if it was about to be given. They sat in the cafeteria drinking bad coffee in the same kind of silence with which they'd been sitting in Dylan's company. Strained enough to make Zac's heart ache. He wanted to help but he couldn't just barge into a space he might not be welcome in.

It was still the early evening of what had been a beautiful day. Harsh sunlight had faded to a soft glow. How much better would it be if they could be sitting on the beach at Takapuna, watching the sunset over Rangitoto? They'd had their first moments of real connection on that beach and surely it would be easy to talk there. Apart from anything else, Summer needed a break from the emotionally traumatic situation she had unexpectedly found herself in. Some way to reassure herself that her life hadn't suddenly gone belly-up. They couldn't go to the beach right now, of course, but...

'Let's go back to the base,' he suggested.

Summer's immediate reaction was to shake her head. 'I can't leave. Not yet.'

But Zac could see the way her gaze went to the windows and beyond. That the notion of escaping was more than appealing.

'Dylan's being well looked after. He's probably going to sleep for hours, anyway. We don't have to be that long but we could get changed and bring our bikes back here and that way we'll be ready to go home later, when things are more sorted.'

Summer looked torn. 'It's a good idea,' she said. 'You should do that. I'd better stay, in case... in case...'

'I'm confident that your dad's not going to die,' Zac said gently. 'You'll be back by the time he wakes up and it can be you that takes Dylan in to see him...if you want,' he added hastily, seeing the way her eyes darkened with emotion. 'Only if that's what you want.'

'I don't. I told him I didn't ever want to see him again. He...I...' Her voice cracked and she dropped her gaze, clearly struggling not to cry.

It broke Zac's heart. Here was this strong, capable and incredibly independent woman in front of him, but he could see a young girl as well. A girl who'd been unbearably hurt in some way.

*Oh... God...*had her father been violent to her? Snatches of memory flashed through his brain like a slide show that could be felt as much as seen. The fist that couldn't be avoided. The fear in his mother's eyes. Blood. *Pain...* The knot of overwhelming emotion in his gut was powerful enough to make him feel ill. There was grief there. And a white-hot anger. He had to move. Standing up, he held out his hand to Summer.

'You don't *have* to see him again,' he said, his voice raw. 'And you're not going anywhere alone.'

He loved the way Summer took his hand so readily. The way she kept moving as she got to her feet, coming into his arms as if it was the only place she wanted to go. He held her tightly, pressing his cheek to the top of her head. More than one group of people in the cafeteria were staring at them. The need to protect Summer kicked up several notches.

'Let's get out of here,' he said softly. 'Just for a bit.'

It was the right thing to do. It was Summer's idea to see if there was an ambulance crew who might be clear of a job in Emergency and have the time to drop them back at the helicopter base and that allowed her to step back into her own world. They changed out of their flight suits into civvies and that made it feel as if the job they'd been to at Piha Beach was really over. Best of all, they kicked their bikes into life and could roar through the city, weaving in and out of the traffic, feeling the freedom of their preferred mode of transport.

No. That wasn't the best of all. This was. Walking into the green space of the enormous park over the road from Auckland General Hospital. Walking hand in hand in soft light, mottled by the canopy of ancient trees, and feeling the caress of a gentle summer breeze.

It was as good as life could get in this particular moment, Zac decided. And then he changed his mind only moments later, when Summer's hand tightened around his and she started to talk, albeit tentatively at first.

'You never knew your dad, did you?'

'No. My mother never even told me his name. The only father figure I had came into my life when I was about four and…he was never a dad to me.' He could have said so much more but this wasn't about his story. Or was it? Would sharing something that was never spoken about be a way of showing Summer how much he was prepared to trust her? How much he wanted her to be able to trust him?

His hesitation made it irrelevant. Or maybe Summer was already lost in her own memories.

'My dad was the best,' she said softly. 'I adored him. Everybody did. He coached all the kids and was the chief lifeguard and a volunteer fireman and the go-to guy for the whole community.'

'Country town?' Zac was absorbing the undercurrent of her words. He could let go of the idea that her father might have been violent and the relief was sweet. But what else could have caused such a catastrophic breakdown in a relationship that should have remained strong for a lifetime?

'A beach community. Tiny. There was never much money but if the sun was shining and the surf was up, it didn't matter. We were all happy. Dad would be running his surf school or the shop and Mum made pots that she painted and sold to the crowds that came in the summer holidays. I had a long ride to school on the bus but that was okay, too. We'd go with salt in our hair from a morning ride and we'd know there'd be time for the sea again after school.' She was silent for a moment. 'I'll bet Dylan's life is just like that. When I saw him on the beach today, he looked like all my friends did at that age. Like I did. I could have guessed who he was before he said anything if I hadn't been trying so hard not to think about who it was we were treating.'

'That must have been so hard for you. I can't believe how well you coped with it.'

Her tone was suddenly shy. 'You helped more than I can say. Thank you.'

Their steps had slowed and now they stopped.

Zac drew Summer into his arms. 'You would have managed anyway but I'm glad I was there. I'm glad I'm here now.'

Summer pressed against him for a long moment but then pulled away with obvious reluctance, shaking her head. 'It's not over, though, is it? And I have no idea what to do. It's all this confused jumble in my head. I've hated Dad for so long. I want to hate Dylan too, but he's only a kid. It feels like he's the cause of it all but he's not. It's not his fault and…and he even looks a bit like me…'

Zac smiled. 'He does. He looks like a cool kid.' His breath came out in a poignant sigh. 'I wish I'd been around then.' He lifted an eyebrow. 'Maybe I was. Did you happen to notice a Combi van full of cool teenagers with their surfboards at your beach?'

It made her smile. 'Lots. Did you happen to notice a cool chick with a pink surfboard? My dad made it for my thirteenth birthday.'

The smile vanished. Those big blue eyes glittered with unshed tears and her voice was shaking. 'I miss him…I've always missed him…'

In the silence that followed, they both sat down on grass that was bathed with the last of the day's sunshine. Zac let the silence continue but then decided that he could ask a question now. He'd been invited into that private part of her life. It felt as if she was ready to trust him but he made his words as gentle as possible.

'What went wrong?'

Summer had picked a daisy from the grass and she held it in one hand. With the fingers of her other hand, she delicately separated a tiny petal from the others and plucked it clear.

'We lived for surfing competitions,' she said. 'They were the big, exciting days over summer and there were always huge barbecues in the evenings. Everybody knew each other and they were big social events.' Another petal got plucked from the daisy. 'There was this woman—Elsie—who turned up to a lot of the comps when I was a kid. Mum said she was an old friend of Dad's but she was weird about it. When I was thirteen—the year I got the pink surfboard—I heard a rumour that there was something going on between Elsie and Dad.'

'Ohh…' Zac knew instantly where this story was likely to go. He closed his eyes as if to hold back the distress of a small family about to be broken apart.

'I asked Dad and he denied it. I asked Mum and she said it wasn't true. She got really angry and told me never to mention it again. Dad had married *her*. He loved *us*. He was ours. For ever. She was always a bit over the top, you know? When she was happy, she was super happy but little things upset her. A lot. I didn't dare mention it again.'

More petals were coming from the daisy. Half of its yellow centre had a bare edge now.

'And then, one day—out of the blue—just after I turned sixteen, Dad told me that he had to leave. That he had to go and be with Elsie. That he'd been living a lie and life was too short to keep doing that. He thought I was old enough to understand, but all I could see was that he'd been cheating and lying for years—to the people who loved him the most in the world. I told him I never wanted to see him again.'

A whole bunch of petals got ripped clear. And then the daisy fell, unheeded, into the grass.

'Mum fell to bits. She wouldn't eat. She never stopped crying. I got her to see a doctor and he put her on medication but it was never enough. The pills got stronger and there were a lot of them. Enough for her to take so many that when I came home from school one day and found her unconscious on the floor, it was too late.'

'Oh, my God,' Zac breathed. He reached for Summer's hand and held it tightly.

'She never came out of the coma.' The tears were escaping now. 'They turned the life-support off a few days later.' Summer scrubbed at her face. 'Dad had the nerve to turn up at her funeral but, as far as I was concerned, he was guilty of murder. I refused to talk to him. Or even look at him. And I haven't, ever since…' Her indrawn breath was a ragged sob. 'But I had to, today. And I thought he was going to die and…and I realised I still love him. And when Dylan told me I'd been mean, I realised how horrible I have been. He tried to keep up the contact. He wrote to me. He rang me. He sent me presents. I ripped up the letters and blocked him from my phone. I sent the presents back. And then, when Mum died, I blamed him, even though I knew that wasn't fair. I'm… I'm not a very nice person, am I?'

Summer tilted her face up and her expression broke Zac's heart. It was easy for it to crack because it had become so incredibly full as he'd listened to her story. No wonder she'd believed the accusations she'd heard about him with regard to Shelley after experiencing the pain that deception and denial could cause and yet she'd been prepared to take his word that the accusations were unjustified.

And how hard must it be for her to trust any man?

But she had trusted *him* with not only the story but her own fear about what kind of person she was.

He had to gather her into his arms.

'You're the nicest person I've ever met,' he said softly. 'And you don't have to do anything you're not ready to do. That includes talking to your dad or taking any responsibility for Dylan. I'll take care of everything.'

He pressed a kiss to the spiky hair that always felt so surprisingly soft. 'I'll take care of *you*,' he whispered. 'I love you, Summer.'

Those words blew everything else away.

It felt as if Summer had been adrift on a stormy sea for the last few hours, in a boat that was being dragged further and further into a storm where it would capsize and she would have no protection from the wild water in which she would inevitably drown.

But those words were an anchor. Something that could prevent the drifting and allow her to ride out the storm and then choose a safe path to find her way home.

They made the pain bearable. They made any doubts evaporate. Zac hadn't tried to defend her father in any way. He understood how hard it had been for her and he was ready to protect her completely. She didn't have to see her father or have anything more to do with her half-brother if that was what she wanted. He would take care of it all.

Those words made her feel safe.

It felt as if her own words had simply been waiting for the chance to escape. To be made real.

'I love you too, Zac.'

It was the moment for souls to touch through the windows that eyes provided. For trust to be offered. For lips to touch gently and linger to seal an emotional troth.

But the safety Zac's words promised gave Summer something else as well.

Strength.

'I think I do want to see Dad,' she said slowly. 'I've let this haunt me for too long. It's been like poison in my life. Probably in my relationships, too. I don't want that any more.'

Zac's smile was gentle. 'No poison permitted,' he said. 'Not for us.'

'I don't want it to hurt anyone else, either. Like

Dylan.' The reminder that there was a scared kid curled up asleep on the couch in a relatives' room was a wake-up call. It was time to get back to reality.

'Let's go back.' Summer's limbs felt stiff as she got to her feet. How long had they been sitting there? 'We need to get stuff sorted. Like where Dylan's going to stay tonight.'

'He could come home with me. Gravy's really good at taking care of waifs and strays.'

'But he's not a waif. He's...he's part of my family.' Her breath came out in an incredulous huff. This was going to take some getting used to. 'I always wanted a sibling when I was a kid. Maybe this could be...I don't know...a gift, even?'

'Maybe it is.'

'So I guess I'll take him home with me. There's room on the boat. Flint will just have to sleep somewhere else.' She frowned. 'Except he might not want to. Dylan, that is. He thinks I'm mean. I suspect he hates me.'

Zac took her hand again as they crossed the road to the hospital entrance.

'He just needs the chance to get to know you. And I have a feeling that sleeping with Flint might be a pretty good place to start.'

'Maybe.' Summer smiled up at Zac as they headed for the lift. 'I think the only point in my favour right now, though, is that I'm your girl-friend. You're the hero who saved his dad. *My* dad,' she added in a whisper.

It still didn't feel real. Her world was still spinning.

It was undeniably weird. But part of that weirdness was very, very good.

Zac *loved* her.

She could deal with anything on the strength of that.

Even this.

CHAPTER NINE

ZAC WAS THE HERO, all right.

It was Zac that Dylan chose to have by his side when he walked into the intensive care unit later that evening to see his father—leaving as much distance as possible between himself and Summer.

It was Zac who drew Summer closer to his other side as they reached the bed that was flanked by a bank of monitors, IV stands and the nurse who was monitoring her new patient carefully. Jon Pearson was awake, but only just. He was still weakened by the massive blood loss he had suffered and the medication for his pain made staying awake almost impossible.

But it was Summer that Jon focused on first when his eyes fluttered open and, for the first time in so many years, she met the eye contact—

and held it. Neither of them smiled. The moment was too big for that.

But it was a start. A new beginning?

A smile appeared for his young son.

'Still got my leg.' Jon's voice was croaky. 'We'll be riding those waves again soon, kid.'

Dylan was clearly struggling not to cry. He inched closer to Zac and lifted his chin but his voice wobbled. 'Your board's munted, Dad. It got chewed to bits.'

'No worries. I'll make a new one.' Jon closed his eyes and drew in a long breath before he pushed them open again. 'We'll put that one up on the wall. In the shop. People'll come from miles around to see it.'

His eyes drifted shut again. The brief conversation had exhausted him. The glance between the nurse and Zac gave the clear message that it was time for visitors to leave.

Zac put his hand on Dylan's shoulder. 'We'd better head off and let your dad get some rest, buddy. You can come and see him again tomorrow.'

'But I want to stay here.'

'Summer's going to take you home with her. On her motorbike. We found a helmet that will fit you back at the rescue base. She's got a cool bike—it's a Ducati. And it's red.'

The smile for Summer made her think of being out on the road with Zac's bike in front of her. Heading off so that they could spend time together somewhere special. The wave of longing was overwhelming. All she wanted to do right now was be somewhere with him again. Doing something that didn't involve such difficult emotional drama. They had only just declared their love for each other. How unfair was it that it was going to be impossible to spend this night in each other's arms?

Maybe Dylan noticed the look that passed between them. Or maybe he just wasn't impressed by the incentive that had been offered. He ignored Summer and fixed his gaze on Zac.

'Can't I go home with you?'

'Hey... I only live in a house. Summer lives on a boat and it's really cool. And she has a dog. His name is Flint.'

'I don't like dogs.' The words were sullen.

It was an obvious effort for Jon to open his eyes again. 'Go with Summer, lad. She's…she's your big sister…'

Another moment of eye contact and this time Summer found a smile, albeit a wobbly one.

'I'll look after him, Dad. You rest.'

It was a promise that wasn't going to be easy to keep, Summer realised a short time later when, thanks to the bike ride, Dylan was forced to make physical contact by putting his arms around this unwelcome newcomer in his life. It felt even harder after Zac's bike peeled away to leave her alone in Dylan's company. He had offered to come back to the boat with them but Summer knew she had to make the effort herself. Maybe it was a kind of penance. Or a need to prove that she wasn't the monster that Dylan believed she was—the unknown other child who'd always been so mean to his dad.

Looking after him in a physical sense wasn't the problem. She could give him a safe place to sleep and feed him. Finding him some acceptable clothes might be more of an ask, but she could sort that kind of issue tomorrow. It was the emotional side of things that was far trickier. Dylan had lapsed back into the miserable silence he'd displayed while they were waiting in the relatives' room. She didn't even have a television to distract him with on the boat.

At least there was Flint, who was overjoyed to have company after a longer day than usual, and feeding her dog gave Summer something to do after a tour of her home that took such a short period of time.

'I'll make us something next. Do you like bacon and eggs?'

Dylan shrugged.

'You'll just have to ignore Flint trying to persuade you that he's still starving. He'd do anything for a bit of bacon rind.'

Sure enough, it was Dylan's foot that Flint laid his chin on when they were eating. Summer pretended not to see a piece of bacon rind being slipped under the table.

'Your bed is usually where Flint sleeps,' she told him, 'but I'll put some clean sheets on it and Flint can sleep somewhere else.'

Another shrug but it was clear that Flint intended to share his bed with the visitor when things were sorted for the night.

'Want me to put him somewhere else? Up on deck?'

'Nah.' Dylan climbed into the bed and edged to one side. 'I'm good. There's room.'

Summer took her hand off Flint's head and got a lump in her throat as she watched her dog step politely into the space provided and then curl up beside Dylan.

It was far too soon to offer the comfort of physical touch herself—for either of them—but Flint seemed to understand that that was exactly what was needed.

'Night, then. Just give me a yell if you need anything.'

A grunt indicated how unlikely that was but, as Summer turned away, she heard a small voice behind her.

'Did Zac mean what he said? About going for a swim in the morning?'

'Sure. Are you up for a bit of jogging, though? Flint will want to come and he can't go on the bike.'

Another grunt. 'Bet I can run faster than you can.'

He could. With his skinny legs and arms pumping, he stayed ahead of Summer with Flint close beside him and only slowed to wait for her when they got to an intersection and he didn't know what direction to take. By the time they got to the beach the first light of the day had strengthened enough to recognise the tall figure waiting alone and Dylan took off, even faster. Summer was a little out of breath by the time she caught up.

'You ready?' Zac asked Dylan. 'It'll be a bit cold.'

Dylan shrugged. 'Guess so. But there aren't any waves.'

He was right. Takapuna beach looked like a giant swimming pool this morning, calm enough to gleam under the rising sun. It would have been perfect for paddleboarding if they'd had more time.

'We get waves sometimes,' Zac told him. 'But this is just a wake-up dip. Last one in is a sissy…'

Maybe it was only Summer who noticed the tiny hesitation that gave Dylan the head start. The man and the boy ran into the sea, splashing through the shallow water and then diving as soon as it got deep enough. With a joyous bark, Flint took off to join them and Summer wasn't far behind.

The water was icy enough to make her gasp. By the time it felt bearable, it was time to get out. She and Zac both had to work today and there was a lot to get organised.

Zac seemed to have everything in hand, however, including towels waiting in a pile on the dry sand.

'Gravy's got breakfast ready. Do you like bacon and eggs, Dylan?'

Summer expected him to say that he'd had them already—for dinner last night—but she saw the way his gaze shifted to Flint, who was shaking seawater out of his coat.

'Yeah...bacon's cool.' And then he squinted up at Zac. '*Gravy?*'

It was such a perfect echo of the tone she had used herself the first time she'd heard the unusual name that Summer laughed. 'She's Zac's gran.'

Zac gave Dylan the same explanation as they headed for his apartment.

'Quick shower, then,' he ordered as they got inside. 'And I'll find some dry shorts for you. Might be a bit big, though.'

That shrug was becoming very familiar. 'Doesn't matter. My jacket's dry.'

The bright red and yellow jacket was the first thing Ivy commented on. 'Are you a lifeguard, Dylan?'

'Yep. My dad's in charge of the surf club. I help with Level One—the little nippers. We teach them about water safety and get them confident in the waves.'

Summer had never heard such a long speech from Dylan. There was something about Ivy

Mitchell that broke through barriers of age or anything else, wasn't there?

'That's something to be proud of,' Ivy told him as she placed a laden plate in front of him. 'It's a wonderful organisation. I *always* swim between the flags.'

Zac snorted. 'You've never waited till the lifeguards are on duty to swim.'

Ivy looked affronted. 'But if I *did*, I'd swim between the flags.'

Zac and Summer laughed and, to her astonishment, a wide grin spread across Dylan's face a moment later. It was the first time she'd seen him smile. Even better, the smile didn't vanish as his gaze met hers. He even shook his head and then rolled his eyes as if to ask if this astonishing old lady was for real.

Ivy made it easy to organise the rest of their day.

'I can take Dylan into the hospital with me,' Zac said. 'And check on him during the day.'

'He can't stay in the hospital all day,' Ivy declared. 'And he needs some clothes. I'll take him shopping.' She winked at Dylan. 'I love shopping.'

'He needs to visit his dad,' Summer said. '... Dad,' she corrected herself.

The look that flashed between Zac and his grandmother told her that Ivy was already filled in on the fragile relationship but she gave no sign of any judgement.

'Of course he does. We'll go in on the bus after we've done our shopping. What do you need besides clothes, Dylan? A phone? Yes... You need to be able to text your dad. And your friends back home. And Summer, maybe, when she's at work.'

'I'll see what I can do about juggling shifts in the next couple of days,' Summer said. She was being excused from spending time with her father today and it felt like a reprieve. Or did it? 'But I'll drop in after my shift to visit and then I can take Dylan home.'

'Good.' Ivy wasn't going to allow for any more discussion. 'That's settled then. For today, anyway.'

'How long is my dad going to be in hospital?'

They all noticed the possessive pronoun that didn't include Summer.

'A fair while, I expect,' Zac told him gently. 'But we'll look after you, okay?'

'I've got a few days off coming up,' Summer said. 'First day's on Friday.'

'I've got Friday off, too,' Zac said. 'And you might be a bit over hanging around the hospital by then. We could do something fun, maybe.'

Dylan was staring at his plate. There was a pile of bacon rind carefully pushed to one side. Summer wondered how he might be planning to sneak it out to Flint, who was lying on the terrace with his nose on his paws, just inside the open French windows.

'Ever tried paddleboarding?' Zac continued.

Dylan snorted. 'Paddleboarding's for sissies.'

'Careful, mate… Summer's the queen of paddleboarding around here. And I'm learning and loving it.'

Ivy's lips twitched. Had she noticed how often Dylan's gaze strayed towards the doors? 'It's

Flint's favourite thing to do,' she said. 'He rides on the end of Summer's board.'

Dylan's jaw dropped. 'No way...'

'Yes, way.' Summer nodded. 'And if you got good at it, he might ride on the end of your board.'

The shrug seemed more like an automatic reflex than something dismissive this time. 'Okay... I'll give it a go. If Dad's okay.'

'Friday's a day or two away,' Ivy said. 'Let's take this one day at a time, shall we? Now, scoot, you two. You've got jobs to go to. Dylan and I need to do the dishes and then go shopping. You'd better give that bacon rind to Flint, Dylan, before Summer takes him home.'

Day by day, Jon Pearson continued to improve after being moved from the ICU to a private room the day after his long surgery. Visiting became less awkward for Summer as she and Dylan got used to each other's company. While he seemed to accept her presence in his life, though, he wasn't in any hurry to share his father. She had yet to spend any time in Jon's company without Dylan being present and there were often others there as well. A steady stream of friends came from the west coast to visit and, in the first couple of days, there was the excitement of the media interest in the survival story of man versus shark. Dylan was clearly bursting with pride for his dad and that meant he spent as much time as he could glued to the side of his father's hospital bed.

And maybe the lack of any private time with her father was a good thing as they also got used to breathing the same air again. It meant that they only talked about safe stuff. Like their jobs. They could swap stories about dramatic incidents or the kind of training it took to be able to do what they did. Dylan was keen to share his own take on dramas at the wild beach that was his playground. He became more and more interested in hearing about Summer's work, too. Especially if the stories included Zac. There was a bit of hero worship going on there and that was fine. Thanks to both Zac and Flint, Summer had something to offer in the way of being a potential part of his family.

Not spending time alone with her father made life easier for now. Not being able to spend time alone with Zac was less welcome. Oddly, though, the lack of physical contact was bringing them closer on a completely different level. One that was making Summer think more about the future. About what an amazing father Zac would make. He seemed to know instinctively how to relate to Dylan. When playfulness was needed. When a word to the wise was called for. Considering that he'd grown up without a father as a role model for himself, it was extraordinary. But, then, he'd been brought up by Ivy so maybe it wasn't so unbelievable.

The time they spent together on Friday felt like a family outing. Jay was happy to provide paddleboards for them all and, fortunately, it was another day with a sea calm enough to make it easy for learners.

Ivy was on her terrace in a deckchair, watching closely enough to wave whenever Summer or Zac looked up at the house. She was paddling slowly, Flint on her board, with Zac and Dylan not far away. Having been kneeling until he got used to the feel of the board, Dylan was standing up now. He had to be getting tired but he was giving it everything he had, trying to keep up with Zac.

'Hey… Flint…' he yelled. 'Come on *my* board…'

'Go on,' Summer urged. 'It's okay. I won't be offended.'

'Come on, Flint.' Zac joined in the chorus. 'Share the love…'

The big black dog obligingly jumped off Summer's board, making it rock. For a short time, all they could see was the black head above the water and then he was hauling himself up onto a different board. But not Dylan's. He had chosen Zac's. The dog was used to the effort it took but Zac wasn't prepared for how unstable it made his board and he lost his balance and fell off. Flint stood on the board, anxiously watching for him to resurface, and then barked in relief as Zac caught the board. Summer and Dylan were both laughing so hard they almost fell off their own boards.

It was a moment she would remember for ever.

Shared laughter that created a bond. A family kind of moment.

Even the mention of it later made them laugh, lying on their towels and soaking up the sun as they rested tired limbs.

'Wait till I tell Dad how you fell off,' Dylan said. 'You should have seen your arms. You looked like a windmill.'

Summer's smile was more poignant. 'He chose your board,' she said. 'I hope you realise how honoured you are.'

Dylan dug his feet into the sand. 'He was supposed to choose mine.'

'He wasn't being mean,' Summer said. 'Maybe Zac's board was just closer.' She held Zac's gaze, though. She wanted him to know that she didn't believe that. That her dog had chosen him because he was his person now, too. As important in his life as Summer was.

That they were a kind of family already?

It could be like this with their own children one day, couldn't it?

Was she ready to trust that much? To give herself so completely to Zac?

Maybe Dylan guessed where her thoughts were going and felt left out. That might explain the glare she could feel that made her turn her head.

'What's up?' she asked. 'You hungry again?'

Dylan said nothing and an echo of what she'd just said replayed itself, the words taking on a new significance. She sighed. Maybe they weren't becoming as close as she'd thought.

'You still think I'm mean, don't you?'

'Just because you go and visit Dad now doesn't make it all right,' Dylan muttered. 'It's just because he's sick.'

'Summer's not mean,' Zac said quietly. 'I don't like hearing you say that, buddy.'

'She was mean to Dad. I saw him crying one day, when I was little. After one of those parcels came back. I heard him tell Mum how much he missed her. How much he *loved* her.' The emphasis was a statement of how little she had deserved it.

Summer's heart ached. How much time had she missed having a father in her life?

'It's going to be different from now on,' she said. 'I'm sorry about the way I acted. I was...'

'Hurt,' Zac finished for her. 'Summer wasn't that much older than you are, Dylan. How would it make you feel if your dad decided he wanted to go away and make another family? With someone else?'

'She could have come too.' Dylan's feet were almost buried in the sand now.

Zac's hand moved discreetly between the towels. Summer felt his fingers close around hers. Offering support. An ally. Telling her that Dylan might not believe she had deserved her father's continued love but *he* did. Telling her that she had *his* love now as well. She had to swallow hard and scrunch her eyes shut so that the full feeling in her heart didn't escape as tears.

'She had to look after her mum,' Zac said carefully. 'Her mum got sick.'

'My mum was sick.' Dylan's voice wobbled. 'She…she died.'

'So did Summer's mum.'

There was something different this time in Dylan's gaze when he raised it to meet Summer's. Almost…respect?

Zac gave her fingers a squeeze and then let go, as discreetly as he'd made the contact. He must have been able to sense how big this moment was but, yet again, he knew how to lighten things and make it seem no more than a natural step forward.

'It's cool living on a boat, isn't it?'

'I guess. But it doesn't go anywhere.'

'It could.' Summer was happy to move away from anything intense. 'The sails aren't any good but it's got a motor. I turn it on every so often to make sure it still goes. I should do it tonight, in fact. I'll let you turn it on, if you like.'

Dylan didn't respond. He had rolled onto his side and was tickling Flint's tummy.

Zac smiled. 'You didn't really mean it when you said you didn't like dogs, did you?'

A skinny bare shoulder gave a single shrug.

Zac's tone was as light as it had been when he'd mentioned the boat. 'Sometimes, when things are tough, we say—or do—stuff we don't really mean. Sometimes it's good to just forget about them and start again.'

They all lay there in silence after that. Silence that made it easy to hear Ivy's call from the terrace above.

'Yoo-hoo! Are you lot coming inside for some lunch?'

They got to their feet and gathered damp towels to shake the sand out of them. Walking up to the house, Zac took Summer's hand. Flint was on her other side with Dylan close beside him.

The boy looked up at Summer. 'Do you reckon Flint'll sit on my board one day, too?'

It was another one of those moments to treasure. Zac's hand was warm around hers. She had her beloved dog by her side and she knew she was about to make her little brother smile.

'I reckon you can count on that. Maybe next time we go out, even.'

* * *

Going out on the boards wasn't going to happen again any day soon. A summer storm was brewing and the next day the wind came up and the sky darkened ominously.

'We'll go and visit Dad after lunch,' Summer said. 'We can go shopping this morning and find him some presents. Some nice things to eat, maybe, seeing as he's feeling so much better. Hospital food's not up to much.'

'Zac said I could go and see where he works and he'd show me some cool stuff. Like the saw they use to cut people's chests open.'

'Did he? Okay…we'll have to see how busy they are in Emergency, though. We can't get in the way if Zac's in the middle of saving someone's life.'

Dylan's nod was serious. 'I wanna do that one day. I think I'm going to be a doctor like him.'

'You could be a paramedic, maybe. We get to save lives too, you know. And being on the helicopter is pretty exciting.'

Dylan's grin was sympathetic. 'Zac gets to do everything. He's the best.'

Summer had to grin back. 'Yeah...I think so, too.'

The best boyfriend. The best lover. And he would be the best father for any children she had.

Oh, yeah...she was so nearly ready to trust that much. Maybe the only thing in the way was to deal with the ghosts still haunting her past.

It was time to talk to her father. Properly.

The opportunity came later that day when Zac appeared during their visit to Jon and told Dylan he could have the promised tour of the emergency department.

'You want to tag along, Summer?' he asked.

'No, I'm good. I'll stay.'

The sudden tension in the room advertised that the significance wasn't lost on anybody. Dylan hesitated, clearly feeling protective of his father. He eyed Summer.

'Is that cool, Dad?'

'It's fine, son. Come back and see me later.'

Summer gave Dylan a smile intended to reassure him that she wasn't about to start being mean. Zac got the message, even if Dylan didn't. His glance, as they left, told her that he was impressed she had chosen to stay and have her first time alone with her father. Proud of her, even?

It was impossible to know how to start. Summer fiddled with the supply of grocery items she and Dylan had chosen to bring in. Fruit and biscuits and ginger beer. She held up a packet of sweets.

'Do you *really* love sour worms?'

'No. But Dylan does.'

'Ah…that might explain the salt and vinegar crisps, too.'

'No. I *do* love them. Might need a beer to go with them, though.'

Small talk seemed to be exhausted at that point. Summer finally sank into the chair beside the bed as the awkward silence grew.

It was Jon who broke it.

'I can't tell you how sorry I am, love. About what happened to your mum. About not being there. I know you think it's my fault that she died...'

Summer shook her head. 'I did, I guess. But I'm a bit older and wiser now. I get that people make their own choices. And I know Mum wasn't the easiest person but...she really did love you...'

'I know that. I loved her, too.'

'Not as much as you loved *her*...'

'Elsie?' Jon's smile was sad. 'That was a very different kind of love. We'd grown up together. We started dating when we were fourteen. We were always going to be together.'

Summer's jaw dropped. 'So why did you marry Mum?'

Jon lay back against his pillows, his eyes closing. 'Elsie's family had moved to Australia and she was a couple of years younger than me. She was going to come back to New Zealand as soon as she turned eighteen. And then we were going to get married.' His breath escaped in a long sigh. 'I was nineteen. Elsie had been away for more than a year and I...I was lonely. Not that that's an excuse but there was this big surf comp and a party afterwards and your mum was there and she…she made it clear how keen she was on me and…'

'And she got pregnant?'

'Yes. I had to tell Elsie and…and she was devastated. Said she never wanted to see me again. It was the worst time. Your mum was in love with me and she said she couldn't live without me and she really meant that. I was scared she'd hurt herself if I left and, besides, there was a baby involved and I wanted to do the right thing by everyone. And then you came along and I found a new kind of love that I thought would always be enough. I didn't think I'd ever see Elsie again but she turned up for a comp when you were about eight or so. And it was still there. The way we felt about each other.'

Summer was silent. How would she feel, she wondered, if she and Zac were forced apart and then she met him again years later? Would she still feel the same way?

Yes, her heart whispered. It would never change.

'We tried,' Jon said quietly. 'And, when it became too hard to stay away from each other, we still tried not to let it hurt you or your mum.'

'Did she know?'

'I think so. But she chose not to believe it. I think she thought that if she simply refused to believe it, it wouldn't be true. Her mental health was always a bit fragile. She had a stay in hospital after you were born with postnatal depression. I had about three months of looking after you by myself and...it might sound horrible but I'd never been happier. You were my little girl and I loved you to bits. I never, ever wanted to make life hard for you.'

Summer had tears trickling down the side of her nose. 'I'm sorry, too. For shutting you out. And the longer I did it, the easier it seemed to just leave it all behind and not go back.'

'Ah...don't cry, love.'

'But Dylan was right. I was mean to you.'

'You were a kid. And you were protecting your mum. That's not something to be ashamed of.'

Jon stretched out an arm and Summer was drawn from her seat and into a hug that took her back in time. Back to before the tragedy of losing her mother. Back to a time when she and her father had shared so many magic moments. Like the moments she had had with Zac and Dylan so recently. The bonding family moments.

They didn't get wiped out, did they? Maybe they got covered up but you could find them again and how good was that?

'I kind of like having a brother,' Summer admitted when they finally stopped hugging and both blew their noses and regained some composure. 'He's a nice kid.'

'He's very like you were at that age.'

Summer smiled. 'Yeah…he's got seawater in his veins, too.'

'Has it been okay—having him to stay?'

'I think he likes the boat. And he loves Flint. And Zac.'

'You and Zac—is it serious?'

Summer's nod was shy. It was as serious as it could be, wasn't it? She couldn't wait to tell Zac about this conversation. About the moment when she knew she had forgiven her father because she recognised that his love for Elsie had been the way she felt about Zac. That being with anyone else would be living a lie.

'It must be getting in the way a bit, having a kid brother on the scene.'

'It's fine. It won't be for ever.'

'It could be a while longer, though. They say I'm healing well but I won't be up on my feet for a week or so and I won't be going home any time too soon. I'm worried about Dylan missing too much school. I've got friends who've offered to have him stay. Parents of his friends.'

'He'd be worried about you.'

'It's not that far. Someone could drive him over almost every day for a visit. If I send him home, he won't be interfering in your life so much.'

It was unfortunate that Zac and Dylan arrived back in the room at precisely that moment. Just in time to hear those last words.

Zac's eyebrows shot up. Dylan visibly paled.

'Are you sending me away?' he demanded.

'I'm just thinking about all the school you're missing. Come and sit down and we'll talk about it.'

'I don't want to go away. I like being here. I like Flint and…and paddleboarding and stuff.' Dylan glared at Summer and her heart sank. She hadn't been included in why he wanted to stay. Of course he must think she'd been complaining about him interfering with her lifestyle but that wasn't true. She needed to talk to him as well. She cast a helpless glance at her father.

'I'll explain,' he said quietly. 'Don't worry.'

But Dylan's face had shut down. He shoved his hands in his pockets. And then he frowned.

'Oh, no…where's my phone?'

'You had it downstairs. You were taking a photo of the rib spreaders, remember?'

'I must have left it there.'

'I'll go and look. I have to get back to work, anyway.'

'I'll come with you,' Summer said. 'And then I can bring the phone back. You stay here with Dad, Dylan.'

It was a relief to be alone with Zac. 'He's got the wrong idea,' she told him. 'I'd said how good it was having him but Dad thinks he's getting in the way of *us* being together.'

Zac's glance as he pressed the button for the lift gave Summer a jolt of sensation deep in her belly.

'I guess there is a bit of truth in it,' she admitted, as the door closed behind them.

'You think?'

They were alone in the lift. Zac caught her chin with one hand and ducked his head to place a lingering kiss on her lips. By the time the lift doors opened on the ground floor, Summer's legs were distinctly wobbly.

Oh, yes...they needed some time alone together. Soon.

'I had the kit open in my office to show him,' Zac said. 'I reckon that's where the phone will be.'

They had to go through the emergency department to get to the office. To Summer's surprise, she heard someone calling her name.

'*Kate*...what on earth are you doing here?'

'I had to come in with Shelley. Felix broke his

leg. It looks like… Oh, it's all such a mess, Summer. I'm so glad *you're* here…'

Kate's gaze shifted to the man by her side and there was no way Summer could avoid this.

'This is Zac,' she said quietly. 'Zac Mitchell.'

The door to the resus area behind Kate opened further and Mandy appeared. Summer could see into the room properly now. A young woman was sitting on the bed. She was crying and she had a small, limp boy in her arms. A boy who had dark curly hair and big dark eyes.

A boy who looked remarkably like Zac?

CHAPTER TEN

A PART OF Summer's brain had frozen.

She couldn't think straight and it was frightening. To be able to do her job, she *had* to be able to think straight no matter how many things were happening at once or how horrible those things might be.

But this was different. This involved a person she was intimately involved with and this time she couldn't step back and try to cloak herself with a clinical perspective, the way she'd been able to do when she had to deal with treating her father.

This was about Zac. And whether she'd been right in following her heart and giving him her trust. It had been given; there was no question about that. It had been given totally in that moment of connection with her father when she'd recognised that the strength of how she felt about this man would last a lifetime.

But even that truth seemed to be outside the anaesthetised part of her brain. Or maybe she couldn't catch it because too many other things were demanding her attention.

Kate had taken hold of her arm and her tone was urgent. 'I tried to call an ambulance but she said she had to take Felix to Auckland General and just put him in the car and took off. All I could do was follow. And now she won't let anyone touch him. Mum and Dad are on their way but...'

Rob was coming towards them, stripping off gloves. 'Right,' he said. 'I'm clear. We've got a two-year-old with a query fractured femur.'

'His GCS is down,' Mandy told the consultant. 'I'm worried about blood loss.'

Rob gave a curt nod. 'Children compensate too well to start with. Let's get a type and cross match stat, in case we need some blood products.'

'Do you need a hand?' Zac's voice was quiet. Calm. It made Summer think of the way she had been when faced with treating her father. At least Zac was managing to function professionally. His brain hadn't frozen.

Rob nodded. 'Hang around for a minute. Just in case.' He turned back to Mandy. 'Has the paediatric orthopaedic team been paged?'

'Yes...' Mandy lowered her voice. 'And we might want to page Psyche, too.'

'What?' Rob was instantly on the alert. 'Why?'

'It's a bit odd. She hasn't let anyone else touch him since she carried him in. She got hysterical when we tried so that's why we got her to carry him in here.'

Rob looked past Mandy. And then took a second look and stepped further into the room. 'Shelley, isn't it? Didn't you work here not so long ago?'

'Hi, Rob. You remember me?' Shelley's tears evaporated as she smiled. 'Not the best way to have a reunion, is it?'

'This is your son?'

'His name's Felix.'

'We need to look after Felix.' Rob moved closer

but didn't try to touch his young patient. 'He's hurt his leg, yes?'

'I don't want anyone to hurt him.' Shelley's hold on the toddler tightened and the child whimpered.

The sound made Summer feel ill. It was the first sound she had heard Felix make and it wasn't the normal cry of a child in pain. She knew to worry a lot more about the quiet ones. Especially when they seemed so quiet and well behaved in a frightening situation. And this injury was serious. She could see how swollen the small thigh was and the odd angle of his lower leg. The colour of his foot wasn't good, either. Urgent treatment was needed.

Kate was still holding onto Summer's arm as she moved closer to Rob so she was forced to move as well.

'There's been a series of accidents recently,' she said. 'Some bad bruises. Shelley said it's because he keeps falling off the new bike he got for Christmas but...'

The look in her eyes said it all. Even Shelley's

own family were suspicious that the injuries weren't accidental.

'Trampolines are dangerous.' Shelley's voice was calm. 'I *told* Mum and Dad he was too young to have one but they went ahead and bought it, didn't they?' She bent her head over Felix and rocked him in her arms. 'It's all right, baby. Everything's going to be all right...' She started humming a song.

Rob stepped back from the bed, his face grim. 'Yep. Page Psyche. And we'll go ahead with treatment without signed consent if we have to. Let's see if we can get an IV in and I want to get that leg splinted properly before we do anything else to try and prevent any more blood loss.'

He turned back to Shelley. 'We need you to sign a consent form, Shelley, so that we can treat Felix. You know the drill, don't you?'

Shelley stopped singing. She nodded without looking up. 'That's why I had to come here,' she said. 'I don't think I can bring myself to sign a form that means you're going to hurt my baby. His father can do that.'

'His father?' Rob looked sideways as if he expected to see someone else in the room but there was only Zac, standing near the door, Mandy, who was wheeling the IV trolley closer, Summer and Kate, who leaned in to whisper in her ear.

'I didn't mean to tell her that Zac was back in the country,' she said. 'It just slipped out...'

'Yes.' Shelley raised her head and she was smiling sweetly, her gaze fixed on Zac. 'That's his daddy. Zac. Dr Mitchell.'

It wasn't just Summer's brain that was frozen now. The whole world seemed to have stopped spinning.

'Oh, my God...' The packages containing the cannula and swabs dropped from Mandy's hands.

Rob's jaw dropped.

'Oh...no...' Kate buried her face in her hands.

Zac simply stared at Shelley, his face utterly blank and immobile.

Shelley smiled back at him, the Madonna-like expression completely out of place given that she was holding her badly injured child.

And then, as if given a director's cue, everybody turned to look at Felix. Still pale and limp, he looked back at all these strangers with those big dark eyes. From a perfect little face that was framed by soft dark curls.

The heads turned again, as if at some bizarre tennis match, to look at Zac.

There was no denying that it seemed quite possible he was Zac's child.

Zac's voice was as expressionless as his face. 'I am *not* his father.'

Mandy made an odd sound as she stooped to collect the packaging. 'But...I remember now. Shelley was always bringing you stuff. Cakes. Even flowers...and...' She straightened and looked at Felix again, her words trailing into silence.

Doubt hung in the air. As palpable as thick smoke.

Summer stared at Zac. The numb part of her brain was coming back to life. Painfully. She had had those doubts herself but she had dismissed them on nothing more than Zac's word.

On instinct. But her instincts weren't always to be trusted, were they?

She'd believed Shelley when she'd first proclaimed the paternity of the baby she was pregnant with and she'd been wrong about that. She'd believed her mother when she'd said that no man could be trusted and that love wasn't enough. That what had gone wrong in her life was her father's fault. She'd been wrong about that too and look at how much damage trusting her instincts had already done.

All she needed now was the reassurance that she was right to trust Zac.

To love him…

But she couldn't see anything. He could have been looking at Rob or Mandy or Kate. Possibly even Shelley. There was nothing there for her to read and, just for a dreadful moment, fear kicked in. A dreadful certainty that there was something he hadn't told her.

What if he *was* hiding the real truth?

And then something happened that forced an abrupt break to that desperate eye contact.

Felix screamed—a tortured sound that gave way to broken sobbing.

Rob spoke briefly to Zac and then gave Mandy a curt nod and took a tourniquet from her hand. It was past time they got some pain relief on board for this little boy.

Shelley burst into tears as well. 'I didn't mean it,' she sobbed. 'It just *happened...*'

Kate moved to touch her sister. 'It's okay,' she said. 'We're going to look after you. *And* Felix.'

More people arrived in the resus area. The paediatric orthopaedic consultant, who had two registrars with her. Another nurse, who was carrying a paediatric traction splint, and an older woman who didn't have a stethoscope around her neck. The psyche consultant, perhaps? Or someone from Social Services?

Zac was edged further back in the room and Summer couldn't catch his gaze again.

She didn't need that reassurance, did she? This was *Zac* and of course she believed him. Shelley was crazy. She wanted to say something but the noise level in the room was rising and the moment had long gone. X-ray technicians were getting ready to use the overhead equipment. Tubes of blood were being handed to a junior nurse. An IV line was in place and medication had been administered. Felix, thankfully, was now sedated and peacefully asleep.

Stuck in a corner behind Kate at the head of the bed, Summer couldn't even move without disrupting something that was far more important than her need to talk to Zac.

'Do you need blood on standby?' One of the ED registrars was by Rob's shoulder as he was getting the splint ready to go on the small twisted leg. Summer had been asked to provide support when they were ready to fasten the Velcro straps and put the traction on to straighten the leg.

'Yes, please. Just in case. Have we got the type and cross match back already?'

'Yes. And it's good that we checked. He's AB negative.'

Summer's brain raced. AB negative was the rarest blood group there was. And she was pretty sure that the parents had to have the blood groups of A, B or AB.

'That means that someone who's an O couldn't be his father, doesn't it?'

Rob nodded. 'You ready?'

'Yes.' Summer lifted Felix's foot, keeping one hand under the calf. The splint was slipped into place and Rob began to fasten the straps. 'Zac's an O.'

The look Rob gave her was scathing. 'You didn't really think he was lying, did you?'

'No. Of course not. But this *proves* it...' But Summer could feel the colour flooding her cheeks.

She'd meant that it was proof for Shelley's family. For the psychiatrist. But she'd made it sound as if *she* had needed the proof. And she hadn't. But Rob didn't believe that. What if Zac didn't believe it, either? She would never be able to erase that last time their eyes had met. When she'd bought into that collective doubt for just a moment in time because she was so sure there was something he hadn't told her. A moment that could potentially have been long enough to destroy the trust they had built between them. Possibly irreparably. And she couldn't blame him entirely if it did.

She had to get out of here. She had to find Zac.

'I'm sorry, but I've got to go,' she told Kate. 'I'll be back later.'

Pushing her way out of the resus room, Summer scanned the emergency department. An ambulance crew she recognised were handing over a patient at triage. Orderlies were pushing patients in beds or wheelchairs. A nurse was wheeling a twelve lead ECG machine into a cubicle. A group of doctors were standing around a computer screen looking at the results of an MRI scan. There were people everywhere but no sign of Zac.

She went to his office. It was empty, but there, on the corner of his desk, was a mobile phone. Dylan's phone. The reason they'd come down here in the first place. The reason they'd had those brief moments in the lift when he'd kissed her with all the pent-up passion of not having been able to make love to her for days now.

And superimposed on those thoughts was the image of Zac's face and the way he'd looked at her that last time. As if he didn't even recognise who she was.

*Oh... God...*was it possible that that kiss in the lift was the last one she would ever receive from him?

Summer clutched Dylan's phone.

She could ring Zac. Or text him.

And say what? That the blood results were back and now everyone believed him? With the unspoken assumption that that 'everyone' included her?

No. This was too big for a message that could be misinterpreted in any way. Too big for communication that couldn't include body language or touch, even.

In the moment of indecisiveness, the phone in her hand began to ring. For a heartbeat, the wild hope that it might be Zac brought the sting of relieved tears to her eyes.

'Is that you, love?'

'Oh… Dad…'

'Dylan wanted to check that you'd found his phone.'

'Um…yes…'

'I need you to take him home. To collect his things. We've had a talk and I've got friends coming to collect him this evening.'

'Okay… I'm on my way. Just give me a minute or two, yes?'

She had to go back to the resus room first. Rob was amongst the team members who were standing back as a series of X-rays were being taken.

'Rob?' Summer tried to catch his attention discreetly. 'Do you know where Zac is?'

'I told him to go home early. To get himself away from this until it's sorted.' Rob's gaze was on Shelley, who was now flanked by two security guards and well away from her son. He shook his head. 'It's always so much worse when there are kids involved in this kind of crisis.'

Indeed it was. And now Summer had a child involved in what felt like a personal crisis of her own. She raced back to her father's ward. Dylan made no protest about being bundled into his jacket and helmet for the ride home and it took all of Summer's focus to cope with the traffic and blustery conditions as she rode over the exposed harbour bridge. Rain wasn't far off now and it could well be accompanied by a thunderstorm by the look of the turbulent sky.

Dylan ignored Flint when they arrived at the boat, which should have been a warning sign, but Summer had too much else on her mind.

'I've got to go and see Zac—just for a minute,' she told Dylan. 'I'm sure he'll want to see you before you go tonight.'

His look was as scathing as the one Rob had given her not so long ago but she couldn't explain why she had to see Zac face to face instead of ringing him. Or to try and reassure him that Zac didn't want him out of the way and not interfering with his life any more than she did. She wouldn't know where to begin, trying to explain any of it to a young boy, and there simply wasn't the time.

'It'll take fifteen minutes. Twenty, tops. You pack up your stuff and, as soon as I get back,

I'll take you back to the hospital so your friends can collect you.'

'Fine.' Dylan turned away from her, the word a dismissal.

It was only a few minutes' ride away but the lower level of Ivy's house had an empty feel to it. Summer kept knocking on the door but the sinking feeling got stronger. Nobody was there to answer it.

A voice came from the balcony above, though.

'Is that you, Summer?'

'Yes.' She stepped back until she could see Ivy peering over the railing. 'I'm looking for Zac.'

'He's not home yet. Come inside and wait for him. This weather's getting dreadful.'

'I can't. I've got to get back to Dylan. If you see him…can you tell him I'm looking for him?'

'Of course.' Ivy pushed wind-whipped strands of hair back from her face. 'Is everything all right, darling?'

Again, Summer had no idea where to begin. She could only nod, emphatically enough to try and reassure herself. If nothing else, the action had the bonus of holding back tears.

If Zac wasn't home by the time she'd taken Dylan back to the hospital and returned, then she would tell Ivy everything. Surely this amazing woman was old and wise enough to be able to tell her how to fix something that seemed to be more and more broken with every passing minute.

It had probably been a little more than twenty minutes when Summer eased her bike into the stand at the marina. She hurried down the jetty to the mooring. Past all the yachts she knew almost as well as *Mermaid*, all of them bobbing on an increasingly disturbed bed of water. Most were empty, waiting for their owners to have some spare time at the weekend. A few, like hers, had people living in them.

Clive was the closest marina neighbour and he was the friend who could look after Flint if she was ever caught out on a job.

He was out on his deck right now, tying things down in preparation for the coming storm. He stopped what he was doing and stared at her, a rope dangling from his hands.

'*Summer!* What on earth are you doing here?'

The odd query stopped her in her tracks. Why wouldn't she be here, on her way to her home?

'I saw you going out. Fifteen or so minutes ago. Thought you must be getting the boat out of the water or something.'

'*What?*'

Summer started running, her boots thumping on the wooden boards of the jetty. She got to the point where Flint was usually sitting to await her return. Beside the bollards that her ropes were always curled around to anchor the boat.

There was nothing there. Just an empty space—the water dark and rippled.

Summer looked out at the harbour. It was already darker than it should be for this time of day. There were plenty of small yachts anchored away from the marina and they were all moving in the wind and the roll of the sea so it took a minute to make sure that none of the movement was as purposeful as it would be if there was anybody on board.

If there was a motor running.

She couldn't see *Mermaid* anywhere.

Dylan had taken her. With Flint on board.

He'd run away.

Thank goodness her brain didn't freeze this time. Summer knew exactly what she had to do. She pulled her phone out and made two calls.

The first was to the coastguard to raise the alarm.

The second was to Zac.

'Summer?' His tone was wary. Had he been reluctant to even answer her call?

'Zac...where are you?'

'I'm at the rescue base. I came in to have a chat to Graham.'

About giving up being a HEMS member, perhaps, so that he didn't have to work with her any more? The thought intruded even if it was completely irrelevant right now—fear for others was overwhelming any fear for herself.

'Dylan's gone. He's taken *Mermaid*.'

'No way… *How?*'

'I showed him how to start the motor last night. And I…' Summer squeezed her eyes shut. This was all her fault. She'd taught Dylan how to make the boat move and then she'd left him alone long enough to give him a head start. She'd known he was upset and *that* was her fault, too. He'd overheard the tail end of the conversation she'd had with their father and he had only been beginning to be ready to share the most important person in his life with the girl who'd been so mean to him for so long.

'There's not much petrol,' she added desperately. 'He could be drifting by now. He doesn't know how to use the radio and he's got Flint on board as well and…' Her voice caught in a strangled sob.

Zac's voice was calm in her ear. Any wariness had vanished. 'Have you called the coastguard?'

'Yes. Of course.'

'There'll probably be a call coming in here soon, then. Monty's on base. I'll ask him whether it's possible to go out in this weather. How soon can you get here?'

Summer was already running back towards her bike. 'I'm on my way.'

CHAPTER ELEVEN

As a doctor, Zac Mitchell knew that a heart couldn't actually break.

As a man, he knew that that was exactly what happened to his heart the moment he saw Summer arrive at the rescue base.

One look into her eyes and he could feel it happening with a pain like no other he had ever experienced.

Of course she was afraid. Her young brother and her beloved dog were out there on an unforgiving sea in a small boat in a breaking storm but—as he held the eye contact for a heartbeat longer—he could see another layer to that fear.

Summer could feel the distance between them.

And she knew why it was there.

She had doubted him. He might love her more than he thought it was possible to love anyone, but how could he commit to spending his lifetime with someone who had doubted him—about *that*—even if it had only been for an instant?

But right now that didn't matter.

What mattered was that Summer needed him and he could be here for her a hundred per cent, even if it would be for the very last time.

He closed the physical distance between them with a couple of long strides and then he gathered her into his arms and held her close enough to feel his heart beating against her small body.

'We'll get through this,' he promised. 'Together.'

The hug was a brief one. They weren't alone, even though most of the day's crew had gone home.

Graham's face was grim. 'The coastguard's boat has been tied up with an incident out on Waiheke Island. They're on their way but conditions are worsening and the light's fading fast.'

'We've got to find them.' Summer's face was white. 'What if they drift into a shipping lane? With no lights?'

The thought of what would happen to a small boat, unseen by a container or cruise ship, was horrific.

Monty looked away from the weather maps and rain radar he had on the computer screen in front of him. 'We'll take the chopper up. Turn on the sun.'

Graham shook his head. 'It's getting marginal for flying.'

Monty's chair scraped on the floor. 'We'd better get on with it, then.'

Summer raced to her locker to grab her gear. Zac was right behind her.

'You don't have to do this,' she told him. 'I would never ask you to put yourself in danger for my sake.'

Zac could only meet her gaze for a moment. 'You would never *have* to ask,' he said. 'And I'm coming. End of story.'

Every minute that passed was a minute too long.

It took time to scramble into the gear they needed for an offshore rescue mission like this.

A titanium undervest and Poly-Lycra under-suit and then the specially designed wetsuit. The life-jacket came equipped with a range of accessories like a strobe light and mini flare, a whistle and a knife and even survival rations.

They strapped themselves into winching harnesses even though they knew how unlikely it was that it would be safe to be winched onto a moving target like a boat in this kind of weather. It took more time for Monty to complete pre-flight checks and get them airborne. And then minute after minute flicked past as they circled the inner harbour, working out from the marina where the *Mermaid* had been moored.

There was no sign of any small craft, including the coastguard vessel. Even the larger ferries were on the point of suspending services and the only people going near their yachts were those who were trying to make them more secure as the storm bore down on the city. The flash of lightning on the horizon heralded the first squall of rain that obscured visibility enough to make Monty curse.

'We'll have to abort if this keeps up.' But there was no indication that the pilot had any intention of calling it quits yet and Summer knew that this was the kind of challenge that Monty thrived on. He'd keep them as safe as possible but would also take them right to the edge if that was what was needed to save a life.

The squall passed and the helicopter rode the rough air to move further towards the open sea. They were over the shipping lane between Rangitoto and Takapuna beach now—the track that the big container and cruise ships took to gain entry to the city's harbour. Fortunately, there was no sign of any large vessels. Unfortunately, there was no sign of any smaller ones either.

'The swell's getting big enough to make it hard to see,' Zac said. 'Turn on the sun, Monty.'

The night sun was a light attached under the nose of the helicopter that had the strength of thirty million candles. Below them, the white foam of breaking waves on the big swells covered the inky blackness of the deep water below.

Summer's stomach sank and then rose with

every air pocket that Monty negotiated. Her heart just kept on sinking. They weren't going to find the *Mermaid*. It would get thrown onto rocks and there would be no way to rescue Dylan. Or Flint.

'There...' Zac's shout was triumphant. 'Nine o'clock.'

'Where?' Summer's heart was in her mouth now. 'I can't see them.'

'Wait...'

The water rolled and, yes...there she was, riding the swell. Still afloat but clearly without power. Being washed towards the rocky coastline.

Monty was on the radio instantly, relaying the coordinates to both the coastguard and the team ready to mobilise on shore.

'Can you get me down?' Summer's hand was already on her harness, her gaze on the winch cable that would need to be attached.

'Bit dodgy...' Monty's tone was a warning. 'You sure about this, Summer?'

'No.' It was Zac who spoke—the word an appalled exclamation. 'I'll go down.'

'The coastguard's not far away,' Monty said. 'They'll be able to get someone on board.'

'My brother's down there,' Summer responded. She surprised herself with how calm she sounded. 'He's just a kid. He must be terrified.' She caught Zac's gaze and held it. Flashing through her head was the memory of the last time they had faced the possibility of a tricky winch job—when they'd been called to that young forestry worker with the chest injury. When the question of how much she really trusted Zac had been raised. When she'd known how much she *wanted* to trust him and she'd wanted the chance to demonstrate that trust. Wanted the kind of bond that could only be forged by meeting—and winning—a life-threatening challenge.

She should have been careful what she'd wished for…

But here it was.

'Please, Zac…' Her voice was almost a whisper but seemed magnified by both the internal microphone system and the desperate plea in her tone. 'I need you to winch me down.'

He didn't want to do it. She could feel the strength of how much he didn't want the responsibility of her life dangling on the end of a wire. Trying to time the descent so that she didn't meet the deck of the boat as it came up on a rising swell. She could break her legs. Get tangled on the mast. Smash her head against the side of the boat...

He could refuse and that would be an end to it.

But he knew how much she needed to do this.

And he had to know she would only ask because she trusted him completely.

'Okay...' The word was almost a groan. 'I'll do it.'

It was possible to lock into his training and keep things completely professional up until the moment when Summer stepped off the skid to dangle in the air below the helicopter. Monty had just as much responsibility for keeping her safe but it felt as if he had her life in his hands.

And he couldn't let anything happen to threaten that.

Right now, the pain of knowing she had doubted

his word was utterly irrelevant. She was trusting him with her life.

And he *loved* her…

How could he have even believed for a moment that he would prefer to live without her in his life?

Nothing mattered other than keeping her safe. Keeping Dylan safe. Even keeping Flint safe because Summer loved him.

And he loved her…

The tense minutes of the descent had sweat trickling down his spine beneath the layers of safety gear.

'Minus six metres.' Summer sounded remarkably calm. 'Five…four…no, five…'

It was so hard to judge with depth perception changed by the artificial light, let alone the heaving sea changing the actual distance. They had to time the swells and wait for the moment when they could—hopefully—get the meeting of Summer's body and the solid deck of the boat exactly right.

And, somehow, they did.

There was an awful moment as Summer fell

on landing and slipped across the sloping deck. It looked as if she would go overboard or potentially get caught and he would have to fire the charge that would cut the cable and prevent the helicopter being pulled from the sky. How had she managed to find a handhold and release her connection to the cable at the same time? But there she was, clinging to a handrail and holding the cable clear as she gave the signal to wind it back in.

'Take it up, Zac...' Her words were a breathless but relieved statement. 'I'm good.' He must have imagined the grin because he couldn't possibly see from this distance, but he could still hear the words despite how quiet they were. 'Thanks, mate...'

And then she disappeared into the interior of the yacht and, only seconds later, the lights of the coastguard boat could be seen approaching. There was nothing more that the helicopter crew could do except provide light as another difficult mission was launched to take the disabled *Mermaid* under tow and get her back to safety.

* * *

It was over.

Every bone in Summer's body ached.

Her heart ached now, too. For a while, she had forgotten the finality of the way Zac had looked at her when they'd been in the emergency department with Shelley and Felix.

Fear had taken over. And then the adrenaline rush of the rescue mission. By the time the *Mermaid* had been safely towed into port, the helicopter had long since landed, which was just as well as the storm had well and truly broken. Dramatic forks of lightning and crashing thunder were a background for getting Dylan safely back to the hospital and his father.

He stayed glued to Summer's side as they walked towards the ward.

'Dad's going to be so mad at me, isn't he?'

'No. He's going to be too relieved that you're okay. Like I am.'

The look that passed between them acknowledged the bond that had been forged under circumstances neither of them could ever forget.

In the moment she had climbed into *Mermaid*'s cabin to find a terrified boy crouched in a corner with his arms tightly around a big black dog and she had put her own arms around both of them for a long wordless hug.

There were more hugs in that hospital room. And words of reassurance from both Jon and Summer that Dylan wasn't being banished. That they were a family now and nothing was going to be allowed to break that.

Yes. A poignant joy had taken over from the fear.

The dramatic start of the storm had settled into steady, drenching rain by the time Summer and Flint were given a ride home by Monty, who had come to pick them up from the coastguard's base.

And it was then that Summer realised she had no home to go to. The *Mermaid* couldn't be towed back to her marina until the weather improved.

'Come home with me,' Monty said. 'We can collect your gear from the boat tomorrow.'

But Summer shook her head. Because the fear had returned. The overwhelming relief that her brother and her dog were safe was wearing off. The joy of knowing she had a real family again was also being pushed into the background. What if she had lost Zac from her life? She hadn't seen him for hours now. Hadn't heard from him either, but then her phone had got wet during that rough ride back on the coastguard vessel and it was completely dead.

As dead as that dreadful message in the look that Zac had given her when she'd been seeking reassurance? As dead as the future she had started to dream of? One that had included children that they would take to the beach and build sandcastles with. Teach them to paddleboard so that they could stand up one day and wave at their great-grandmother, who would be watching from her deck.

Ivy...

The yearning for the kind of wisdom and warmth and humour that only Ivy Mitchell could dispense was suddenly overwhelming.

'I need to go to Takapuna,' she told Monty quietly. 'Down by the beach. I'll show you which house.'

The rain was so heavy that both she and Flint had runnels of water cascading off them by the time the knock on Ivy's door was answered.

Not by Ivy.

It was Zac who wrenched the door open but that was all he did. He simply stood there, staring at her. She could see the breaking tension in his face. Relief. *Love...?*

'For heaven's sake, Isaac...what are you *thinking*? Get them inside...' Ivy tugged her grandson away from the door. 'Come in, darling. Oh, my goodness. You're completely *soaked...*'

Flint stayed where he was as Summer moved.

'You too,' Ivy ordered and Flint stepped cautiously onto the polished floorboards, puddles gathering under every paw. 'I'll get towels. Isaac, take Summer downstairs to your place. She needs a shower.' She waited until they were both at the head of the internal staircase, Summer's hand tightly encased in Zac's. 'And a proper hug,' she called after them. 'Don't forget your manners. I'll see you both in the morning.'

It was an instruction they should both have been able to laugh about as soon as they closed the door to the rest of the world behind them but neither of them was even smiling.

Zac pulled Summer into his arms and held her so tightly she couldn't breathe.

'Don't ever scare me like that again,' he growled. 'I thought…. Oh, my God…I thought I was going to lose you.'

It didn't seem to matter that he was getting wet. Or that she couldn't breathe. The hope that this meant Zac still loved her as much as she loved him was enough to survive on. Summer never wanted to move. She wanted to feel his heart beating against her cheek like this and feel his arms around her like the strongest, safest protection ever.

It was Zac who released the hold enough to move and see her face.

'Are you okay? You didn't get hurt?'

'I'm fine.'

'And Dylan?'

'He got the fright of his life but he's okay, too. He's with Dad—waiting to get taken back to the west coast tonight.'

The breath that Zac released was a long sigh. 'And Flint's good. He'll get dried off and we'll be lucky if there's any bacon for us at breakfast. That's all that matters.' His mouth quirked into a crooked smile. 'I'm not sure what Gravy meant by a "proper" hug but a hug is not quite what I'm thinking about right now.'

Summer's gaze dropped from those gorgeous dark eyes to the mouth that she loved almost as much. Her eyes drifted shut as her lips parted to murmur agreement but the only sound that emerged was a whimper of need as Zac's lips found hers.

And, for a very long time after that, the need for a shower or anything else was completely forgotten.

It was a time for a reunion—both physical and emotional. A time to celebrate a bond that could survive testing times and only become deeper.

Stronger.

A time for the kind of honesty that provided the glue for that kind of bond.

'I'm sorry I doubted you,' Summer whispered in the quiet hours of the night, as she lay in the warmth of Zac's embrace. 'It was only for a moment.'

'You weren't the only one.'

'Everybody knows the truth now. And I don't think it was about Felix that made me feel that way. I just couldn't help feeling that there was *something* you hadn't told me.'

'There was.' Zac was silent for a long moment. 'Because it's something I've never told anyone. Nobody knows, except for Gravy. I don't even like thinking about it.'

Summer waited out the new silence. Only her fingers moved where they lay splayed on his chest—an almost imperceptible caress of encouragement. She was being invited into possibly the most private part of Zac's life, here.

'It wasn't the accusation that I was the father of Shelley's baby that shocked me the most,' Zac told her. 'It was the idea that I could have pushed her down any stairs. My stepfather...he was abusive. Violent. I could never hurt a woman. *Ever...*'

'I know that,' Summer said softly. She pressed her lips against the soft skin close to her face. 'I couldn't trust you any more than I do now. I love you so much.'

'Not as much as I love *you*.' Another soft sigh escaped Zac. 'So much I can't begin to find the words.' He moved, bending his head so that he could place another tender kiss onto Summer's lips. A kiss that was enough to move them onto a new space. One that accepted the past and made it part of a foundation instead of a barrier.

'Gravy's got a dream,' he told her then. 'She wants to live long enough to throw confetti at our wedding and drink too much champagne at the reception. She wants dogs tracking sand into the house and babies playing in the garden and on the beach. She even mentioned a paddleboard or two propped up by the shed.'

'Ohh...' Summer was smiling but she could feel tears gathering in her eyes.

Tears of joy.

'You like that idea too?'

The question was almost shy.

'It sounds like the best idea *I've* ever heard.' It seemed an effort to draw in a new breath and it seemed as if the whole world was holding it with her. 'Do you?'

She didn't really need to ask. She could feel the answer in the way Zac was holding her. The way he pressed his lips against her hair.

But it was still good to hear the words. So, *so* good...

'I don't think I could come up with a better one.' But then his voice took on a wicked edge as his lips found hers yet again. 'Or maybe I can,' he murmured. 'Just for now...'

* * * * *

MILLS & BOON®
Large Print Medical

April

The Baby of Their Dreams	Carol Marinelli
Falling for Her Reluctant Sheikh	Amalie Berlin
Hot-Shot Doc, Secret Dad	Lynne Marshall
Father for Her Newborn Baby	Lynne Marshall
His Little Christmas Miracle	Emily Forbes
Safe in the Surgeon's Arms	Molly Evans

May

A Touch of Christmas Magic	Scarlet Wilson
Her Christmas Baby Bump	Robin Gianna
Winter Wedding in Vegas	Janice Lynn
One Night Before Christmas	Susan Carlisle
A December to Remember	Sue MacKay
A Father This Christmas?	Louisa Heaton

June

Playboy Doc's Mistletoe Kiss	Tina Beckett
Her Doctor's Christmas Proposal	Louisa George
From Christmas to Forever?	Marion Lennox
A Mummy to Make Christmas	Susanne Hampton
Miracle Under the Mistletoe	Jennifer Taylor
His Christmas Bride-to-Be	Abigail Gordon

MILLS & BOON®
Large Print Medical

July

August

September